# Trades of the Flesh

FAYE L. BOOTH

# Trades of the Flesh

**TOR®**

A TOM DOHERTY ASSOCIATES BOOK
NEW YORK

TRADES OF THE FLESH

Copyright © 2009 by Faye L. Booth

Originally published in the United Kingdom by Macmillan New Writing, an imprint of Pan Macmillan Ltd.

A Tor Book
Published by Tom Doherty Associates, LLC
175 Fifth Avenue
New York, NY 10010

www.tor-forge.com

Tor® is a registered trademark of Tom Doherty Associates, LLC.

ISBN 978-0-7653-6630-6

First U.S. Edition: March 2011
First U.S. Mass Market Edition: April 2012

Printed in the United States of America

0  9  8  7  6  5  4  3  2  1

*For "Plaguey" Jen, who shares my passion for history's seamy underbelly, and in loving memory of Rosie, who I miss more and more with each passing day*

## Acknowledgments

For their help and encouragement following the publication of my first novel, *Cover the Mirrors*, and/or during the creation of this, my second, I owe my heartfelt thanks to:

- My family, particularly those of you who make it to the end of this book without disowning me. (I jest, of course.)

- My friends, especially Debbie, Jen, and Fatma (test readers extraordinaire), Shelley for double-checking my facts on the human cadaver, and Claire, who never seems to tire of hearing my writing-related meanderings.

- Kim Wilkins for the gorgeous cover quote for *Cover the Mirrors*.

- Jacquelyn Warner, who expanded my collection of art dolls by capturing Lydia's likeness in clay.

- Everyone who has had the kindness to let me know that they've enjoyed my work so far. It still feels weird and wonderful!

- And last but not least (as the cliché goes), to Will Atkins and all at Macmillan, and Edwin Hawkes at The McKernan Agency, for believing in my tales and working to bring them to others.

All men think all men mortal, but themselves.
　　—Edward Young, *The Complaint: Or, Night-Thoughts on Life, Death and Immortality* (1742)


You can see to what intensity of individualism I have arrived . . . for the journey is long, and "where I walk there are thorns."
　　　　　　　—Oscar Wilde, *De Profundis* (1905)

# *Prologue*

## 1887

The late afternoon sun hung low in the sky, warming the muck in the gutters and releasing a pungent stench. Lydia Ketch hardly noticed it as she scurried through the tightly interwoven Preston streets and towards the place she called home, a rented cellar in a filthy boarding-house. The strap around her neck was digging into her, weighed down by her wooden tray of boot and corset laces. She made her way cautiously down the steps, and as she ducked in through the rotting front door of the boarding-house, she kicked a clump of horseshit off her boot.

"Ma?" Ducking into the room she shared with her mother and sister, Lydia blinked in the sudden darkness. No sense lighting a candle until all three of them were home. The thick scent of last night's spent wax hung in the air as she made her way over to her mother's pallet bed. Nell Ketch stirred as her eldest daughter's shadow fell over her, and winced at fresh pain.

"What time is it? What're you doing back?"

"I told you I'd come to check on you, didn't I? I'm going back out, though, keep your hair on."

Nell hawked and spat yellowish slime onto the floor at the side of her straw mattress.

"Sold much, then?"

Grudgingly, Lydia shook her head. "I'll go over the station; might do better there. Plenty of people." She jumped as she felt her mother's birdlike fingers close around her wrist. Nell had never been one for sentimentality, nor had Lydia.

"It'll be tonight, Lydia. I want you to fetch Annabel from school and get away from here."

"Ma, this is ridiculous. I know you don't want us weeping and wailing over you—God knows you've told us often enough—but now you tell me you don't even want us here?"

Nell struggled to sit up, failed, and flopped back down onto the mattress. Her eyes glittered with impatient anger.

"Don't be so bloody soft, girl. I'm doing this for you two, can't you see that? If you're here when they find my body—or worse, if you're cloth-headed enough to fetch them from the parish to come and collect it—they'll take the both of you into the workhouse. Is that what you want?"

Lydia stood in silence, regarding the shrunken heap of skin and bones that had once been her formidable mother. Now all she could recognize of her was the worn, cracked parody of Nell Ketch's voice that she spoke in.

"No. Well, I don't think so." Lydia had been very small when they left Preston Union Workhouse, and she recalled very little of it, save for the vast dining-hall the inmates ate their meals in and the dull grey expanse of yard she had worked in for her keep, collecting baskets of stone chips from around the feet of the men who broke them up. It had been in a corner of that yard that Lydia had found her friend Jimmy, huddled in a ball and clutching at his stomach.

"That's why I'm telling you now," Nell snapped, the sharp edge of her voice slicing through Lydia's thoughts and regaining her attention. "I never was much of a story-teller, and there's enough folk around here whingeing about how bad they've had it. Are you telling me that you'd work till you dropped just to have a bed no better than the one you share with Annabel now, and a couple of bowls of pigswill a day? That you'd graft until you kicked the bucket in one of their wards, sleeping two to a bed with a pox case? You were born in a bed no bigger than this one, but I were still sharing it with another woman. Her babby were strangled before it were born; cord round its neck. You were small and all; I didn't expect you to live." Nell sniffed thoughtfully.

"Don't reckon anyone else did, now I think back. You ended up being called Lydia after the woman I was sharing the bed with. She was Lydia, or her Ma was. Or her aunt; I forget. She suggested Lydia, wherever it was she got it from, and it seemed as good a name as any. Anyhow, what I'm saying is, you don't want to go back to the workhouse."

Lydia shook her head. She hadn't lost the few memories she had of the place, nor of the house her mother had worked in as a scullery maid after they were bought out by a rich man to work in his kitchens. He'd soon given them the boot when he found out about Annie, though. Even the lowliest servant and her brat could see how strained his relationship with the missus was already.

"Just as well Annabel came along when she did," Nell was saying. Lydia gritted her teeth; she'd heard this a thousand times.

"First time I'd been free in years, when he turned me loose. She got his brains too; she'll do grand one day. Make sure you keep her in school; no dragging her down to the station to flog laces with you, you hear?"

"I've promised you, what more d'you want?" Lydia snapped. "I wouldn't dare take Annie out of school: between her griping and you haunting me, I'd never hear the end of it."

"Think, girl. It's no use you promising me anything to keep me quiet now if it's all just wind. D'you think you'll be able to keep the two of you on the money you make?"

"I've done all right so far, haven't I?"

"Aye, but I was out there working and all, until not so long ago. You won't make enough from laces to get a place to live, for starters. You won't even be able to afford this pigsty."

"I'll do something," Lydia sighed. Even the tightness she felt in her throat at seeing her mother so near the end couldn't entirely eliminate the rising anger she felt at Nell's nagging. She was beginning to wish that she'd gone and worked the station instead of coming home.

"Get yours and your sister's things together, then," Nell said. She was curling in over herself, pressing her fists into her guts. "Annabel'll be coming out of school soon, and I don't want to see either of you back here."

Lydia stomped around in the dark, stuffing a few items of raggy clothing into her lace box. It felt heavier than ever now, hung around her neck like a stone. She turned and faced her mother for the last time, unsure as to what she should do. For a moment, Nell's fading eyes met Lydia's own, and Lydia waited for her to say something.

"Annie's got her wits, and they'll do her proud one day," Nell croaked eventually. "But right now it's your turn to use what you have. You've no learning, but you're comely enough in your way."

Lydia blinked, but understood. She didn't say a word.

"Go and get Annabel," Nell said again. "Get your-selves somewhere safe before dark."

Lydia turned on her heel and lugged her lace box out into the hall.

With her eyes fixed firmly on her boots, she slammed straight into Jem Holloway, the local dustman—a bright-eyed lad, popular with the girls and with a repertoire of jokes as dirty as his working clothes—and her box of laces tipped up, spilling smocks and skirts and neatly looped laces all over the cobbles. Lydia swore and dropped to her knees, picking up the laces first before they could stain, while Jem scooped the clothes up in his blackened hands, and handed them back to her. As she watched Jem's grubby hands adding yet more dirt to one of her raggy skirts, she paused, her mind racing.

She thought of the local cotton mills and the heavy machines and the air thick with dust inside them. She thought of the street-sellers who prowled Fishergate, shov-ing each other out of the way every time they spied some-one who looked as if they could afford to part with a pittance for a few pins, and of the matchgirls whose faces had been made monstrous by phossy jaw. Most of all, she thought of the biting cold air on her fingers as she had toddled around the workhouse yard with Jimmy picking baskets of broken stone, and after that, of the house she and Nell had been living in when Annie had come along, where she'd slaved from before the sun came up to well after it went down at night, doing all the jobs deemed too dirty or unpleasant for the other staff.

"Oi, d'you want these or not?" Jem was kneeling beside her, proffering the dropped clothes. With a word of thanks, Lydia took them and stuffed them into her box, then turned and looked into Jem's face, her lips pursed in thought.

"Thank you," she said again. Gripping Jem's wrist, she pulled him down a narrow alley, and looked over his shoulder as he took her up on her silent offer. A grunt of appreciation as he pushed in told Lydia that he hadn't been expecting a virgin, and she wriggled determinedly, pushing herself further onto him. Better to master the trade first, after all.

# 1

## 1888

Lydia awoke to the sound of falsetto protests from the room next door. She poked her nose out from under the thick winter bedsheets and grimaced at the cold of the November morning. Reaching an arm out to grasp the good wool shawl hung over the headboard, Lydia huddled into it, wrapping up as warmly as she could before forcing herself to throw the covers back. Padding across the room in bare feet, she flung open her dress box and dug out a clean red dress—a deep wine-red, not a gaudy cherry: Lydia knew that men with money liked to pretend that the girl they'd just paid a pound to fuck had some class about her. Next door, the creaking of the bed was becoming frantic, and Daisy's breathless claims of innocence rose in pitch with it. She must have had enough of this one by now; he was certainly taking his time to finish.

Catching sight of herself in the full-length mirror facing her bed, Lydia reached for her hairbrush. Her last man had left late the previous night, and she couldn't be bothered to yank the pillow tangles from her hair. She had slept in her corset; it was too much trouble for either Lydia or most of the chaps to fuss about with.

"Lydia?" Annabel's voice, through the noises coming from Daisy's room. "Lydia!" Annie was indignant about something. Probably just running late for school again. Pulling a handful of coloured underthings from her second clothes chest, Lydia dressed hurriedly. She tucked up a little of her skirt to expose her petticoat as a mark of her trade, pinned it with the gilt crown brooch she'd bought from a cheap-jack one night—it made a change from just tucking her hem up, as many of the other girls did—and set off downstairs, tugging leftover knots from her wild brown locks as she went.

Down in the kitchen, Annabel was pulling books out of her pack and complaining that she would miss the school bell. Her cheeks were flushed, and her hair—a warm golden brown, rather than hazelnut like Lydia's—clung to her forehead. Kathleen Tanner, the abbess and owner of the house, was shouting over her, asking if she'd done the washing.

"It's in front of the fire, there, isn't it?" Unlike the

parlour and the girls' bedrooms, which were luxuriously papered and furnished to imitate the picture Kathleen had in her head of quality homes, with fires burning in every grate, the kitchen was sparse and cold, with white-washed walls, a grumbling old range cooker and a long butcher's table of scrubbed wood in the middle of the stone floor, with two wooden benches for the girls to sit on and eat their meals at.

"Not that washing, clot—the sponges! Have you washed them and all?"

Annabel wrinkled her nose.

"Yes, they're soaking in the bucket. Mary's took ages to come clean."

"That right?" Kathleen mused. "Wonder if we'll get anyone coming through from out of town? We might be able to pass her off as a virgin."

"Come off it," Lydia scoffed. "Who's going to believe Mary's a virgin?"

At the sound of her voice, Annabel turned. "Lydia, have you got my exercise book?"

Lydia yawned. "Yes. I borrowed it last night; thought I'd practise my reading."

"You might've told me! I do need it today, you know."

Lydia shrugged. "I'll fetch it now."

"Hurry up," Annie complained, "I'm late enough as it is."

"Then why didn't you get me up earlier?" Lydia yelled over her shoulder as she made her way back upstairs.

"As if I ever get a chance! I'm elbow-deep in a bucket of your dirty linens of a morning, and your linens are grubbier than most."

"You know our deal." Kathleen's voice faded as Lydia stomped up the last few steps and back into her bedroom. "Your sister earns her keep in her bed and you earn yours in the rest of the house. I ain't running a charity here." The rest of her words were drowned out by the sound of heeled boots on the stairs. Annie's racket must have got Mary up.

When Lydia flounced back into the kitchen, she flung out an arm in suitably theatrical manner and started reading from the lesson Annabel had copied into her exercise book.

"*'A foolish woman is clamorous; she is simple and knoweth nothing.'*"

Sitting at the kitchen table eating her breakfast, the sleepy-eyed Mary Fallon giggled. Her golden tresses were immaculate, but then the ones who visited Mary rarely rode her roughly. Things tended to work the other way around in Mary's room: she was known locally as Mistress Birch, thanks to her skill with a cane.

"How very true," Annabel said petulantly. "Now give me back my book."

"*'For she sitteth at the door of her house, on a seat in high places of the city.'*" Lydia smirked back at Mary. "Hold on, this is my favourite bit: '*. . . and as for him that wanteth understanding, she saith to him, "Stolen waters* *are sweet, and bread eaten in secret is pleasant.*"'" The girls laughed.

"Yes, yes, very funny," Annabel said, snatching her book from Lydia and stuffing it into her pack.

Kathleen tutted. "I need you to pick us up some bread and some oil on your way back from school." The abbess rummaged through her pockets and produced a shilling—she hated to put anything on the slate, however small.

"You don't need to go to school to learn how to be a governess," Mary gasped in mock horror. Her lilting accent—Armagh by way of Albert Dock—was deceptively light. "All governess work is is book-learning and knowing how to use a cane, and you've spent enough time reading books." Pushing her breakfast plate away, she stood up and snatched a wooden spoon off the table, bringing it down fast through the air with a practised stroke that whipped past Annie's arm by barely an inch. "I'll make a governess of you."

Annabel flicked the spoon out of Mary's hand, and it clattered onto the stone kitchen floor. "And wouldn't that be grand?" She dropped Kathleen's shilling into her pocket and buttoned it closed. "I'm going to school. Miss Treadwell won't just pretend to hit me if I'm late. I'll be back this afternoon."

"After you've picked up my shopping," Kathleen reminded her. Annie nodded impatiently and made her way out into the hall.

"Your Miss Treadwell couldn't hold a candle to me,"

Mary called after her. "That's why I get paid for floggings and she has to teach the likes of you."

The front door creaked as Annabel opened it. There was a brief pause, then Annie's clear, girlish voice drifted back into the kitchen.

"And I'm sure Miss Treadwell's been crying herself to sleep, Mary. See you all after!"

Lydia grinned and sat down to her bacon and egg. Nobody could say that Kathleen Tanner didn't give her girls enough to keep their strength up, and Annie was always careful to overcook Lydia's bacon until it was brown and crispy, the only way she could eat it. Out in the hall, a heavy, male footfall was making its way to the front door. The kitchen door opened, and Daisy Carter joined Lydia and Mary at the breakfast table. The familiar smell of the trade hung freshly around her, and Kathleen bent her head over her coffee cup and inhaled the brew's strong, rich scent.

"That one were early," Lydia said through a mouthful of egg white.

"Just as well," Daisy replied, gingerly reaching up and feeling the top of her blonde head for bruises from the headboard. "If I'd started any later, I'd have lost the best part of the day."

Kathleen set Daisy's plate down on the table in front of her.

"I thought your visitors just hiked your camisoles up, did the deed and went on their way?" Mary remarked.

"They do, usually. But this one had had a few glasses, I think."

"So that's what your ravished princess act was for, then," Lydia said.

Daisy nodded. "Well, I ain't got all day."


As it turned out, the day was a quiet one. The rest of the morning and the early hours of the afternoon passed without a single visitor to the house. Kathleen, an enterprising Yorkshire woman in her late thirties, had invested a substantial sum in keeping the house presentable both inside and out, and in feeding and clothing her three girls carefully so that they could command the best prices.

Men wouldn't pay to shag a bedraggled little gutter-rat, Kathleen had told Lydia on the night she and Annabel had shown up on her doorstep a year ago; they could get that sort of thing for free. Lydia's shapeless smocks and torn linen had long since been burned, save for one particularly ugly grey dress that she'd hidden in the bottom of one of her clothes boxes. In the early days, after Lydia had finished with some bloated, ugly or foul-smelling man, she would snatch a moment to herself and pull out the raggy old dress to remind herself of the exchange she had made. In many ways, her life couldn't be more different from that of most other seventeen-year-old girls with her background. She ate well, dressed in lovely clothes that the old Lydia Ketch would never have dreamed of wearing, and slept under a safe roof at night, and by now she did not expect to feel even the cheap, fleeting thrill she'd felt when she had Jem Holloway break her in. Nowadays, Lydia was well versed in ignoring the men on top of her, underneath her and inside her. The worst were those who expected her to look into their eyes and tremble like a maiden on her bridal night. Having mastered the act, she understood why moneyed folk often compared actresses to whores.

"Well, there's no sense in the three of you sitting around here all day," Kathleen said as she straightened the sign in the parlour window that offered (not entirely without truth) *Beds to Let*. "You can go for a drink if you like, but if you do catch any men, make sure you bring 'em back here. Don't go far; if we get any coming here I want to be able to get hold of at least one of you."

The girls, sprawled over plush velvet-covered sofas and padded armchairs, lazily reached for shawls and boots, which lay scattered around the room. Regardless of the time of day, the parlour was always lit by gas lamps, thanks to the thick burgundy velvet curtains that were always drawn over the windows, keeping out the light. Flimsy white lace curtains never seemed to be enough for Kathleen: once the house door was shut, the world outside was barred entry, except for those who were prepared to pay the price.

"Can't you sort 'em?" Mary asked cheekily.

Kathleen swatted at her with the paper clutched in her hand. Newspapers weren't the only local publications, and a local printer, Stanley Stoker, known to those in the trade as "Stan the Frenchman," did a nice little sideline in papers for men: ones with lithographs of scantily clad girls, information on the local lasses in the trade and vivid stories detailing the sort of exploits Lydia had become well used to in her year at the house. When she had a quiet afternoon, she often sneaked upstairs to her room with a paper or two and used those stories to practise her reading, and sometimes to make an attempt at writing a story of her own. Kathleen had told Lydia that Stan the Frenchman was in fact an Englishman born and bred, but if you went to him and asked him for some of his "French" papers, he could see you right. Kathleen monitored those particular papers closely for any favourable mention of her house or her girls, keeping an assortment in the parlour to amuse visitors while they waited.

"I stopped 'sorting 'em' the day I had enough to buy this place," she said. "When you've got a house of your own, you can do the same."

"You don't want Mary starting up an introduction house of her own, though, do you, Kathleen?" Lydia cut in. "You'll lose all the whipping boys to her." But they all knew that when Kathleen suggested setting up their own houses, it wasn't a genuine invitation. Far from it—

even if their crotchety abbess was a darling compared to those who kept their girls hooked on opium and in fear of hired punishers if they tried to flee.

"Aye," Daisy said, spying one of her ribbons on the end table and looping it into a bow in her hair, "best keep her sweet, I'd say." She smiled radiantly, and it only added to her innocent appearance. A slip of a thing—something which never failed to amaze Lydia, given the amount of food she had seen the girl put away—Daisy always looked fragile, as if a strong wind could blow her over to Halifax.

"Oh, get out," Kathleen sighed in mock impatience. "Go and bother the folk in the Bull."

Round the corner and barely a stone's throw away from the introduction house, the Old Bull pub was already humming with people taking a glass of ale, or gorging on the publican's wife's pies rather than going home for dinner. In a froth of skirts, hair ribbons and flashes of petticoat, Lydia, Mary and Daisy made their way through into the taproom and jostled their way to the bar. Even in the short time it had taken to walk from the house to the pub, a wintry frost had chilled the girls to the bone, and Lydia breathed a small sigh of relief to be safely inside, where the heat from the taproom fire and the crush of the Bull's patrons could melt through the cold. The

familiar, comforting smell of ale and tobacco smoke gave
her a pleasurable glow.

Over on the good side of the pub, a pair of well-
dressed ladies—travelling, most likely—stared at the
girls. One eyed Lydia's burgundy dress, while the other
flushed and broke her gaze to stare at the grain of the
wooden floorboards.

"Three gins, Alice," Mary said to the barmaid, nam-
ing the drink of whores and suppressing a smirk at the
shock on the ladies' faces. Mary didn't even like gin.

"You smile too often to be intimidating, Mistress Birch,"
Lydia remarked as they took their drinks and pushed
through the press of people crowding the taproom.

"Not when I've got them over the bench, I don't,"
Mary replied. "Ah—table, over there."


The Bull was busy, as it was most afternoons. One of
the bigger pubs, it was handy for the girls to slip out to,
whether to catch a bit of trade or just to get a drink.
Lydia had learned to drink spirits in her first weeks at
Kathleen's, and now she had a certain appreciation for
the harsh perfume of liquor. Still, Kathleen watched the
girls very carefully for any sign that they were getting
rather too fond of it, and preferred them not to drink the
strong stuff at all when they were in the company of men.

"They'll pay more for class," she was constantly saying.

The abbess had been all in favour of Annabel teaching Lydia to read, and Lydia did not need to ask how reading would help to bring the men in. She knew that there were plenty of men who would pay to hear her read certain tales. Now she cast her eyes around the taproom and paused, squinting at the headline spread across a patron's newspaper. *The Fiend Kills Again.* She grimaced at her companions and nodded in the direction of the man with the paper.

"What?" Daisy asked. "The Ripper again?"

Lydia nodded. "How many's that, now?"

"Five," Mary said, gulping down the last of her gin and grimacing at the taste. The liquor left an oily trace around her glass. "I think we should avoid southerners altogether; at least until they catch the monster."

"I don't think Kathleen would appreciate that," Lydia said. "Besides, the Ripper's busy in London, ain't he? If fellows come up here, they come up for business—cotton or something. And we're not street girls; they seem to be the ones he cuts up. He'd never get a chance at our place: one scream and we'd all be in there. Unless it was Daisy, of course. We're used to that."

"Funny bugger," Daisy sniped. "But you do have a point. As long as we don't take men anywhere other than the house, we'll be fine."

"I wouldn't stay out in this weather, anyway," Mary said, huddling closer to the fire. Her skin flushed quickly, and she held her fingers out to the flames. "Too cold."

"I still don't understand why you do that," Lydia muttered into her glass.

"Because I can." Mary grinned.

"But don't you get less for it? If they don't get the room and the bed and all?"

Mary leaned closer, her voice a whisper. "I don't do that for the money, clot! I just do it if I want to, and the chap can't afford me, or doesn't want all that nonsense I do with the cane. Haven't you ever done it for free?"

Lydia thought back to last year, with Jem in the slum sidestreet.

"Aye, once. But I've not had a mind to for a while now."

"That's fair enough." Mary pulled a face. "Not been many good pickings around here for a long time. By the time they can afford us, most of them are old and ugly. At least the street girls and the dollymops at the docks get the sailors."

"And the pox," Lydia pointed out.

Daisy pulled a face. "Mmm. Sailors are dirty things. Besides, who'd be a street girl or a dollymop? One's out in all weathers and getting a pittance for her trouble, and the other's forever looking over her shoulder in case she sees someone she knows from her other job."

Lydia nodded and took a belt of her gin. "Imagine that—you could be serving a fellow tea in someone's parlour in the morning, and on your knees in front of him come nightfall. 'Course," she added with a grin, "you'd have to look up at his face before you'd recognize him."

"Hold up," Mary said, shushing the other two, "I think we've got rivals for lowering the tone of this place." She jerked her head in the direction of a group of men sitting a few tables from their own, and Lydia strained to listen over the din.

"Why, in God's name?" one of the men was bellowing, his speech slurring despite the deliberate effort he seemed to be putting into it. "What would be the sense of it? A man's pleasure is understandable; he must spend his seed and continue his name, but of what use would it be for the Creator to afford a woman the same?"

"I do not claim to understand why, Thomas, but the facts speak for themselves, as countless men in our profession have already confirmed through studies of their female patients. One does not have to explain the presence of the cli—" Here the speaker, whose face was obscured by one of his companions' heads, broke off and lowered his voice, ". . . of the clitoris to know that it is there."

"I wouldn't worry about keeping your voice down, Henry," the man called Thomas said dismissively. "I'd put five pounds on it that nobody in here has a damned clue what you're saying." A group of navvies passed by him at that very moment, all gaudy kerchiefs and exposed shirtsleeves, and Thomas visibly shrank in his seat. Lydia laughed.

"Oi, Jack," she called across to the man hulking over the trembling Thomas. "Made your pound yet?" Daisy and Mary cackled—Lydia had been tormenting Jack with this joke for a while. He'd never have the few shillings spare to pay Kathleen for the use of her room, never mind Lydia's price on top of it.

"Who can afford the likes of you? How can something that was put on this earth for free cost so much?"

"You'll never know," Lydia replied, with a feigned sigh. "More's the pity for you."

"Ah—there we are!" The voice of Thomas's companion drifted across. "A perfect opportunity for each of us to prove his case, is it not?"

One of the other men at their table laughed. "That's an imaginative experiment, Henry, I'll grant you."

"Are you disputing my intentions as a man of science?"

Craning her neck, Lydia spotted him: a clean, neat-looking man, dark-haired and dark-eyed; dressed well in severe black, but smirking like the young lads who tried to catch her eye on the street. He set his glass of port down on the table, and Lydia's gaze trailed up his clean fingers and over his arm. It had been too long since she'd seen a man she could take a fancy to, and she found herself hoping he had a pound to spare.

The man called Thomas turned and looked at the girls. "Oh, come now, Henry. One can hardly apply the same principles to . . . to women such as these. I was referring to the majority."

"And how do you suggest we test *them?*" Henry scoffed. "We'd be clapped in the cells for assault. One must work with what one has available."

Mary rolled her eyes at the backhanded compliment.

"Hmm." Henry surveyed each of the three girls in turn. "House girls, certainly. Your employer's fees aside, I'd estimate perhaps . . . a pound?"

"Goodness," Lydia giggled, "he's right, and it's been a full two minutes since I said it were a pound meself. I believe we're in the presence of a genius, ladies."

"A genius with a lot of spare time and money on his hands, it seems," one of the men at Henry's table chuckled.

"Such is the life of one who has qualified." Henry grinned and stuck his hand out across the tabletop to his companion. "I can't say fairer, can I, Thomas? If you are concerned about the type of woman in question, then we are closer to our mark here than we would be with streetwalkers, and we avoid throngs of angry fathers and brothers on our doorsteps. Shall we say that the loser pays the winner's costs?"

Thomas and Henry shook hands, while the more astute of their companions argued over the third girl.

"So," Henry said, standing and throwing on a thick black overcoat, "lead the way, ladies."

"It's not far," Lydia said. Her eyes chased down the polished buttons of his waistcoat, and she hoped he didn't go for fair girls.

"Henry Shadwell," the man said, passing his case into his left hand so that he could offer his right to Lydia. She took it, somewhat startled—she couldn't remember the last time anyone had done such a thing. Henry kissed the back of her hand through her lace glove, and Lydia marvelled at the effect of such a casual caress, given those she was so used to.

If Kathleen was pleasantly surprised when the girls piled back into the parlour of the introduction house with a man each in tow, she was too shrewd to show it. Mary had, in her unerringly accurate way, quickly identified one of Henry and Thomas's companions as being, in her words, one of her boys, and had soon snared him with a disdainful glare. Lydia had once asked her how she did it, but Mary passed it off as a God-given gift. Kathleen bustled around, taking her four shillings for the use of each girl's room and offering the men a seat and a drink while the girls slipped into the kitchen to fish their sponges from the bucket—Lydia's with a red ribbon attached, Daisy's with a blue, and Mary's with a green. They took turns to soak them in the dish of olive oil left out for the purpose—Kathleen was a firm believer in oil to keep disease at bay. She had once told Lydia that the abbess of the house she had worked in as a girl had been too mean to pay the extra money for olive oil, and so

Kathleen and the other girls there had had to use dripping instead, which congealed far too quickly and made the bedrooms smell like butchers' shops. Wiping the olive oil from her fingers, Lydia smoothed down her dress and strolled through into the parlour.

Henry and Thomas were still locked in earnest debate, while Mary's catch (whose name she hadn't bothered to ask) flicked through one of Kathleen's papers, entitled *The English Vice*. Lydia hid a smile. This one was a good match for Mary; she might make a regular of him, if he had the money.

"But how can metritis be attributed not only to intercourse and self-abuse, but also to abstinence?" Henry was saying. "Surely this is a contradiction in terms?"

"If you are certain that you understand the Lord's most mysterious creation so well, then prove it," Thomas replied, raking Daisy with his gaze. "I'm not paying to argue with you; I can do that for free elsewhere."

"But of course." Holding the door open for Lydia, Henry swept his arm in a courtly gesture, indicating that she should lead the way. She did so, relishing the sound of his boots echoing on the stairs behind her.

"And if the results are inconclusive?" Thomas asked from further down the staircase.

Close behind Lydia—so close that she could feel his breath stirring her hair—Henry laughed.

"Afraid you will not find your mark?"

Mary's visitor laughed, and Mary told him to be quiet.

Then they reached the landing, and each girl led her man into her room, shutting the door behind them. Lydia looked across to where Henry was kicking his boots off. She turned the sheets down.

"Anything fancy?" She smiled mischievously as she looked across at her prize. He definitely had a thing for clothes. Nell Ketch would have called him a dandy, despite his black clothes and carefully trimmed hair and beard. This was a man who paid lip service to respectability to heighten the joy of flouting it; that much Lydia could tell. In one short year, she'd learned more about men than a lifetime of marriage could have taught her. She smiled inwardly as Henry threw off his overcoat, revealing a waistcoat with scarlet-embroidered edging. He grinned as she loosened the bodice of her dress.

"No, nothing unusual. Or at least, not from you." His smile broadened at Lydia's quizzical expression. "You'll see."

Crossing the room, he hooked an arm around Lydia's waist and pulled her close to him. Taking hold of her wrist, he drew her hand down so that she could obligingly caress him through his trousers. She found herself hiding a genuine smile as Henry tensed under her touch, and she lightened her pressure, revelling in the wordless exclamations of lust that rumbled in his throat. With quick fingers, Henry picked the lacing at the bodice of her dress apart, while Lydia slipped the buttons on his trousers open, her expression one of rehearsed casualness as each little metal circlet popped tantalizingly free from its buttonhole. She looked into his face—something she couldn't remember ever doing without it being asked of her—and silently revelled in the tension that lay in his dark eyes and on his trembling lips.

When he pushed her back on the bed, she instinctively parted her legs so that he could kneel between them. But once he had reached up her petticoats and pulled down her coloured drawers—as much a mark of her trade as her pinned-up dresses—Henry did not lean straight over and enter her, but instead pushed her skirts up around her waist, slipped his fingers between her legs and slid them against her, up and down in an ever-quickening motion, causing Lydia to writhe under his touch and look, startled, into his face, where a tiny smile was starting to play around the edges of his mouth. Faster and faster his fingers moved against her, until she felt her heart racing and the echoing rush of blood in her ears. Her body moved without her consent, her hips arching up to press harder against Henry's fingertips, her cheeks flushed with a sensation she had never felt before. The sounds of the house—the creaking of beds, the crack of Mary's cane, even Kathleen's occasional movements downstairs—seemed to fall silent, and all Lydia could hear was the thudding of her heart and her breathless gasps. As the sensation became almost unbearable, Henry dropped forward onto her and fucked her in the way she was more than used to. This time, however,

Lydia's moans of pleasure were real enough, and as Henry spent himself, she realized that she had locked her legs around his waist as if to prevent him from pulling out. When he did not move, but lay on her for quite some time afterwards, she did not object in the least.

# 2

"So, then," she said, when he finally rolled off her and started to button his flap, "where on God's earth did you learn to do that, and why d'you pay to do it?"

Henry looked offended, but Lydia was starting to get the distinct feeling that, for him, such displays of emotion were rarely sincere, but staged for purposes of wit.

"Why, did I not look like I took pleasure in it?" he asked. "I'd have thought that certain signs never lie, to one in your profession." Raising an eyebrow, he slipped his last button into its hole.

"I didn't mean that, as well you know," she said impatiently. "I meant what you were doing before. Do you always do that when you've paid a girl?"

"Not always, but I've never had any complaints. And I had my wager to win today, after all."

"Is that what it was about?"

Henry nodded. "Thomas and I are surgeons; we've been practising for five or six years now. When we happened to encounter you and your friends in the pub, we were debating something of a contentious issue in medicine at the moment, and that is what our bet was based on. You won it for me, so thank you kindly on that score." He tugged playfully at a length of Lydia's hair. "I wonder if Thomas has managed to prove my point further with your friend?"

"Daisy? She's in the room next door, but I didn't hear anything; did you?"

"No," Henry said, "but then I wasn't listening. I was far too busy with the task in hand."

Lydia laughed. "So your bet with this Thomas, this big medical debate, is all about whether or not men can make women . . ." She paused, trying to find words for what it was she meant to say. "Well . . . spend, I suppose?"

"Not just whether men can make them do it, but whether women can indeed experience the kind of climax you just did. Until quite recently, scientific opinion held that it was quite impossible, and unnecessary, and, might I say, unseemly. Some of us question the matter now, and that was where the wager came in. I am of the opinion that the female body is certainly capable of receiving pleasure as well as giving it, and that is what I set out to prove."

A squawk of pain drifted across the landing, and Henry raised an eyebrow.

"Mary," Lydia explained. "I expect t'other bloke who was with you is feeling a bit tender by now."

"Really?"

"Didn't you know your mate was into all that, then?"

"He's not a mate as such," Henry said, pulling on one of his boots. "More of a student. I teach some anatomy to the local apothecaries and barbers. I'm not supposed to, but then I do a lot of things I'm not supposed to do. Still, I'll be sure to have some fun at his expense when the opportunity presents itself." He chuckled quietly.

"Didn't you see him in the parlour?" Lydia asked. "Reading *The English Vice*, I mean?"

"Pardon?"

"*The English Vice,*" she said. "It's one of them gentlemen's magazines, the sort that have stories and drawings of lasses in them. *The English Vice* is one they do specially for the whipping boys, and Kathleen gets it for the parlour—that and a few others. Sells some of them, too. Mary keeps a scrapbook of stories for when I teach her to read."

Henry smiled. "You can read?"

"Yes. My little sister goes to school and she taught me. I'll be ready to teach Mary soon."

"Good Lord," Henry said. "So what made you want to learn?"

"I can learn to read if I want to, can't I?" Lydia said. "Yes, I'll probably end up reading that sort of stuff mostly, but I could look at other things, couldn't I?"

"Sorry," Henry replied in an indifferent tone. "So, by other things, I presume you mean the Bible and ladies' home journals and the like?" He grinned, and Lydia had to laugh.

"I could teach those ladies things that no paper could," she giggled.

"Well, quite," Henry replied. "Perhaps you could write and offer yourself as a contributor."

"On second thoughts, maybe I should just stick to the gentlemen's papers," Lydia said. "I could use a fake name and write wonderful reports of meself." She looked across at Henry, his dark hair tousled and his clothes slowly returning to a state of decent array, but he seemed distracted, his expression thoughtful. Looking back at her, he ran his gaze from the top of her head to the tips of her stocking-clad toes.

"I wonder . . ."

"Wonder what?" Lydia said, pulling herself from her languid admiration of her handsome companion and narrowing her eyes. "What is it?"

"Just a thought," Henry said. He finished tying his bootlaces and reached for his jacket. "Come on. Let's go and talk to your abbess."

. . .

Henry's colleague Thomas was already downstairs in the parlour when they walked in. Henry smiled smugly. Thomas's reluctant shrug told Lydia that he knew he had lost the bet, and he rummaged in his pockets for the money to pay Henry. Lydia found that she was almost annoyed that, in effect, it was not Henry's own money that had paid for her. Then she wondered why such a thing bothered her. Mary's hapless victim sat very gingerly in a chair on the other side of the room, suppressing a wince every time he moved.

"Care for a drink before you leave, gentlemen?" Kathleen asked. All men were gentlemen in her parlour.

"Actually, I'd like a word with you, if I may," Henry said, gesturing to the door as if he owned the place. Kathleen shrugged and followed him and Lydia out into the hall.

"I can't afford to lose any of my girls, if that's what you're thinking," Kathleen said, before Henry could speak. "The three I've got are good, and none of them are leaving to become mistresses."

Henry blinked. "Goodness, no. I'm sure Lydia would be worth every penny, but they would be pennies I do not have—I'm a surgeon, not a physician."

Lydia, hidden by the curtain of her musky-smelling hair, realized she was pouting.

"Lydia tells me that you keep some of the, ah . . . *'local publications'* for visitors."

Kathleen nodded warily. "Why d'you ask?"

"I was just wondering—do you have any of the more recent styles of pictures? The photographic images?"

Kathleen pursed her lips. "Pictures of girls, you mean?" Pausing, she shook her head. "It don't matter, anyway, Mr. Shadwell. I'm selling, not buying. I have my supplier."

But Henry shook his head. "No, I'm not selling them, at least not directly. The fact of the matter is, Mrs. . . ."

"Tanner," Kathleen cut in. She was no more married than Lydia was, but like all abbesses she seemed to have been granted the honorary title. She had once told Lydia that it was because she was like an abbess in a Papist nunnery—married to her work.

"Mrs. Tanner," Henry continued. "The fact of the matter is that I do have a sideline in supplying images to some of the newer papers, as well as certain establishments around the town. Your supplier, for instance—would I be correct if I were to guess that you are referring to Mr. Stoker?"

Kathleen nodded grudgingly, and Henry continued.

"I thought as much. The same people who buy the papers he prints also purchase my photographs. But that, of course, requires models. I was hoping that you would be able to spare Lydia occasionally so that I might capture her image . . . for the right price, of course."

"You take those pictures?"

Henry nodded curtly. "Yes, I have rather an interest in the new photographic technology. The camera I have now is quite wonderful—one of the best around. And there's good money in capturing the likenesses of girls like Lydia, as I'm sure you can imagine." Henry's penetrating gaze fell on Kathleen, and Lydia watched intently.

"As I say, Mrs. Tanner, I am not a man of means by birth, nor am I really one now, in any true sense. What I do have comes from mastering skills and learning to satisfy demand, and I'm sure you can understand that. And the demand for these sorts of pictures is growing all the time: many men consider themselves collectors. An acquaintance of mine, for one. We went to school together, and he lives in Manchester now—he has a library of material, and acts as a distributor on occasion, so I can ensure that the photographs I take will be seen by those with an interest. And they're all waiting for pictures to buy, Mrs. Tanner."

Kathleen's strong gaze, which had seen off many a drunken, penniless lout or an irate pox case, wavered slightly, and Lydia shuffled her feet.

"So," the abbess said, looking back into Henry's face, "what would our terms be?"

"I propose to pay you four shillings per session—the same, I would point out, as you would receive if I hired Lydia for the usual purposes. Lydia and I could then work out a fee for her services between ourselves; again, much as we would do in the normal scheme of things. If I am successful in selling the pictures, then more sessions will be required. Any increase in my fortune from selling Lydia's image would therefore result in an increase in your own. I'll even throw in some copies of the pictures, if you like. Lydia has told me about the collection you keep in the parlour, and I am certain that they would . . . *whet the appetite*, if you understand me." Henry drew himself up straight, and Lydia knew that he was fully expecting Kathleen to accept his offer. What would be the sense in not doing, when she could make the same money from Lydia without her wearing out the bed, dirtying her linen or using oil?

Nodding, Kathleen held out her hand (she wouldn't dream of spitting into her palm when striking a deal with a customer), and Henry gripped it. Lydia watched the sinews in his fingers tighten, and she remembered their slithering movement between her legs.

"Done," the abbess said. "So, will it just be Lydia you'll need, then?"

Lydia suppressed a chuckle. Kathleen was an eternal opportunist.

"For the time being," Henry replied, turning to Lydia. "I'll drop by at the end of the week—Friday, if that's acceptable—to collect you. Wear something nice."

"All my girls dress well, Mr. Shadwell," Kathleen pointed out.

"Oh, I have no doubt, Mrs. Tanner," Henry said

coolly. "But experience has taught me that so many models think only of how they will look out of their clothing, and assume that there is no demand for pictures of young women who are at least partially dressed. Lydia will be perfectly fine if she wears what she's wearing now."

With her stomach rolling giddily, Lydia had to admit that perhaps she was hungrier for a handsome face than she had thought. Until now she had been somewhat baffled by Mary's girlish fancies for lads she encountered in the pubs. Why give something away that you could sell for a good price?

But as she eyed the smooth line of good fabric running over Henry's chest, Lydia thought that perhaps Mary's passions were not as strange as she had thought. With a ghost of the strange tingling Henry had given her, she found herself hoping that he was not planning on their rendezvous on Friday being purely an artistic assignation.

Behind them, the front door rattled, and the bell chimed idly as Annabel pushed past it, her book bag in her arms. The loaf Kathleen had requested poked out of the top of the bag, along with the slender neck of a bottle of oil with a glass stopper.

"This is my sister. The one I told you about."

Kathleen looked somewhat surprised, and Lydia couldn't blame her: she had surprised herself. She'd never introduced Annie to a man before; never mentioned her to them, in fact. Part of her feared that they would assume that Annabel was available to them. A young virgin would be all the more appealing. But there was another reason, too: she had no intention of letting them get to know any more about Lydia herself than they needed to, and what they did know was quite enough. Now, looking somewhat bemused under Henry's detached gaze, Annie looked at her sister as if she'd gone quite mad.

"Oh!" Kathleen said, recovering. "There's an idea! Perhaps we could arrange a trade, Mr. Shadwell. In exchange for the use of Lydia, you could offer our Annabel here some instruction in anatomy. She's a very bright girl, you know . . ."

Lydia was used to hearing her younger sister's virtues extolled—first by her mother, now by Kathleen, even if the abbess did have little time for Annie in the normal run of things.

". . . And Lord knows it'd be handy to have someone in the house with some medical understanding," Kathleen finished. Even Annie's eyes were shining brightly at this. Her hunger for knowledge was a powerful thing.

"So we could arrange a part-payment, if it would be agreeable to you . . . ?"

"No," Henry said. Annie looked as if she had been slapped, and Lydia glowed inwardly. It was a ridiculous notion, anyway—why would Henry raise up a whore's sister as his rival?

"Well, I understand your reticence, Mr. Shadwell," Kathleen said, a touch haughtily. The abbess hated to be denied anything—it didn't sit well with her image of wealth and independence. "But if your concern is that Annabel will be rivalling your own practice, I assure you that any skills you impart will be used solely within these walls."

"I am sure they would be, Mrs. Tanner, but that is not my reason for refusing. I do teach anatomy to suitable pupils, but I do not wish to bring a young girl into the life of a medical practitioner. If young Annabel were worldly enough to understand, she would thank me for refusing your request, believe me." He reached into his jacket pocket and retrieved a gold card case. "But should you ever need my services, please do contact me." Henry offered one of his cards to Kathleen, who took it with a grudging murmur of thanks and stuffed it into her skirt pocket.

Annie flushed, as much in embarrassment, Lydia suspected, as in anger at Henry's denial of her suitability. The elder Ketch girl drew herself up straight, smoothed her dress down the well-developed curves of her breasts and hips, and revelled in Henry's exclusive attentions.

"It's all to the good, anyway," Annie said petulantly. "I've had a new position offered to me, and I intend to take it, so I would not be here to receive lessons from this gentleman anyway, nor have the time to attend them. I leave at the end of the week." She bristled like a cat on a fence.

"What d'you mean, Annie?" Lydia gasped, forgetting

Henry Shadwell for a moment. "Where the bloody hell are you gadding off to?"

"Language, Lydia," Kathleen said automatically.

"Don't look so shocked," Annabel replied. "I'm near fifteen; a lot of girls start looking for places at my age. I've been taken on as a governess for a quality family."

Still reeling, Lydia gaped at her sister. "A governess?"

"I'll be teaching the family's twin daughters. Well-educated girls are always needed to help bring young ladies up correctly."

"And what do you know about being brought up correctly?" Lydia shouted. "I know you want to better yourself, Annie, but you can't climb straight out of the streets and expect the quality to hand their brats over to you."

"I don't think I've done badly, considering the circumstances," Annabel hissed. "What would you have me do? Stay in this whorehouse and wash your linen for the rest of my life? Or perhaps you'd prefer me to get down on my back along with you?"

Kathleen went white with rage, and Henry excused himself and walked back into the parlour, as if he had forgotten something. As soon as the door had closed behind him, Kathleen grabbed a handful of hair from the scalp of each Ketch sister and banged their heads together.

"What have I told you about keeping the tone in here? I am not running some fleapit 'whorehouse' here, and I will not have cat-fights in my hallway, and *especially* not in front of a man, d'you understand me?"

The girls nodded sulkily, all the while throwing poisonous looks at one another.

"In your own rooms, and so long as there's no blokes in earshot, I don't care what you do, so long as Lydia don't end up scratched and bruised. But if you ever try that again, you'll both be out. Got that?"

Annabel huffed and set off upstairs towards her attic room, and Lydia heaved a deep breath before following Henry through into the parlour, refraining from pointing out that foreheads had a tendency to bruise when slammed into each other.

On Thursday night, as the house fell quiet, Lydia sat cross-legged on her rumpled bed and thought about her day, and her appointment with Henry the next morning. The light of a single candle on the bedside table broke the darkness only slightly: the last one had been bashful about getting his clothes off with the lamps on, and Lydia, who had been trapped under him for five minutes that felt like fifty, couldn't really blame him. Now she pulled back her covers and yanked the sheet off the mattress, before bundling it up and throwing it in a corner. Annie hadn't done her rounds this evening: she was supposed to collect all the dirty sheets and give out fresh, and Lydia didn't envy her the rage that Kathleen would no doubt fly into when she found out.

She kicked her drawers over towards the crumpled sheet, and smoothed her hand down the back of her under-petticoat. Satisfied that it was clean enough, she reached around her back for her corset laces, loosening them little by little until she could unhook the front of the garment. Sighing as her body swelled gently out of the restraints of her underclothes, she curled up in the middle of the bed. Once she'd made herself comfortable, she pulled a wool blanket around her shoulders and immersed herself in thoughts of Henry Shadwell and his surgeon's fingers, and picture-papers and the money he had promised her if she posed for him. Mentally, she combed her dress boxes for her favourite things: the damson drawers with lacy frills across the buttocks, the corset that tightened her waist just that little bit more than the others, and her ribboned garters. Perhaps she would wear her burgundy dress again tomorrow; Henry had liked it well enough, and the dark hue made Lydia's skin look all the paler.

A faint knocking—more like a scratching, really—at her door made her jump; she'd almost drifted off in her plans to pretty herself up as much as possible for tomorrow. The door creaked open, and Annie's face peered around it, puffy with disturbed sleep. She'd hardly spoken to Lydia since their scrap, except to tell her to get her filthy boots off the clean parlour rug.

"Can I come in?" Her voice was a whisper, and she didn't sound angry.

Lydia nodded silently, and Annie hurried into the room, pulling her shawl around her shoulders. Lydia patted the bed beside her, and offered her sister a blanket.

"I'm sorry we quarrelled," Annie whispered. "I got a message at school today: my new employer's going to send his driver out for me tomorrow morning." She shivered and pulled Lydia's blanket tighter around her shoulders. "I don't want us to part on an argument."

"Me neither," Lydia sighed. "But when did this governess thing come about, Annie? You never said nothing before."

"I didn't want to say until I was sure, and I didn't want Mary cracking any more jokes; I'm sick to death of the same ones again and again."

"She don't mean to upset you," Lydia said sleepily. "It's just her way."

"I know there's no real harm in her," Annie whispered. "But she's too loud, and you're half as bad when you're with her. We never talk like this when Mary's about."

Lydia shrugged. "So where are you going, then?"

Annie looked into the candle flame, and the profile of her face glowed in the orange light. "To a solicitor's home. Mr. Hollingworth, I think his name was. He has nine-year-old twin girls—they did tell me their names at school, but I forgot. Began with Ls; funny-sounding. They live close to his office, and he works on Winckley Square, so they must be doing well."

Lydia nodded and started to force her fingers through the tangles in her hair, pulling out the worst of the knots. Suddenly, a thought occurred to her.

"They don't know, do they?" Guilt tainted the edges of her voice. "About where you're living now, I mean." She worried at a particularly stubborn knot in her hair. "And what I do."

Annie shook her head. "I don't think so; I don't think even Miss Treadwell knows. It just seems to be our set who know what you are."

Lydia nodded silently. Perhaps it was vain to expect that all of Preston had heard of her.

"What about the girls, then? How will you manage with younger children—you've always been the baby yourself."

"I don't know," Annabel admitted, yawning. "I suppose I'll have to, won't I? And at least they're girls. I wouldn't know where to begin with boys."

Lydia said nothing for a while. Out on the landing, the grandfather clock ticked expectantly.

"So when do you leave? I'll try and make sure I'm free to see you off."

"Ten o'clock," Annie replied. "I've got my things packed, it didn't take long."

"Well, at least you get a carriage instead of having to take the omnibus. That's none too shabby." Lydia forced a smile, and her sister smiled nervously back at her.

"Hold on," Lydia said. "Exactly where are they picking

you up? You won't have asked them to come here, will you?" She already knew the answer.

"No," Annabel admitted. "I said to pick me up by St. John's."

Lydia had to laugh. "Well, you might as well go all the way. It's probably wise: your new boss has probably had his driver bring him here once or twice." As soon as the words were out of her mouth, she regretted them. Moreover, she hoped more than anything that she was wrong.

Annie cringed. "Don't say that. I can't think about that now; I won't be able to get it out of my head. The things I've heard you and the others talking about—I still hear them sometimes! I feel like everything I know is written across my forehead, and that anyone who looks at me will see it straight away." Her voice had taken on a wild air of distress, and she took a deep breath before continuing. "But now I've finally got respectable work. That part of my life is over."

*Go on then*, Lydia thought to herself, *keep your petticoats out of my muck. At least my work kept us alive for the past year—"respectable" or no.* But as she looked at Annie, pale in the candlelight, with trembling lips and eyes glittering with tears, she chided herself for always reacting in temper.

"You'd best go and get some sleep," she said, pushing Annabel's hair behind her ear. "Can't have you falling asleep in the carriage, can we?"

# 3

Annabel eventually agreed to let Lydia help her carry her trunk to the church, but not without making her promise to hide when the driver arrived, and scrub off her paint and unpin her skirts for good measure. She had even insisted that Lydia leave her shawl at Kathleen's (it smelled of scent, or so Annie had claimed). But as the two girls lugged the wooden tea chest up the road, Annie had to concede that she'd never have managed it by herself.

"I didn't think it would be such a problem," she panted.

Lydia hefted her side a little higher. "I didn't think you had so many things."

"Books, mostly, and the school got funds from the parish charities to buy me a couple of decent dresses, not that I think this one'll be decent by the time I get there."

Lydia eyed Annie's outfit, a dull navy creation in wool. "Oh, aye. Hadn't realized that was new." She growled under her breath as the trunk banged into her calves. "Look, try lifting the box up onto your hip for a bit . . ."

It was with some relief that she finally dropped the box onto the path outside the parish church. It was even colder standing in the looming shadow of the great stone building, and the wide steps that led up to the church door were coated with a fine layer of frost. Lydia's legs ached after hauling Annie's chest up the path, but, after a glance at the icy steps, she decided she would stay standing, shifting from foot to foot and rubbing her arms through her sleeves in a futile bid to keep warm.

"You will let me know how you're keeping, won't you?" she said finally. Her teeth chattered as she spoke, and Annie, huddling into her new shawl, nodded in reply. She exhaled heavily, and her warm breath formed a milky mist in front of her face before melting away into the cold of the morning.

"I'll not be fifteen minutes' walk away," she protested, in an airy tone of unconvincing casualness. "To hear you talk, anyone would think I was leaving the county."

Lydia, who had been staring enviously at her sister's

woollen shawl, turned her face up to look Annie in the eye.

"You might as well be. I can't exactly drop in on you once you've moved in there, can I? I don't imagine you'd thank me if I did."

Annabel was silent, and Lydia looked back down at the invitingly thick pile of the shawl.

"I'll get word to you somehow," Annie promised, "even if I have to send you a letter."

Lydia stifled a bitter laugh. Her sister would be in the same town, and yet she was prepared to pay the penny for a stamp every time she had news. Was she really such a social leper, even to her own kin?

"Oh God," Annie murmured, looking out into the road where a small carriage was ambling to a halt, "he's early."

Lydia reached for her sister's hand and squeezed it. "You know where to find me."

Annie nodded, biting her lip. "I know." To Lydia's surprise, Annie leaned over and hugged her, before pulling back and straightening her shawl. "I'll write to you soon with the address. Quick—he's getting closer!"

Lydia ducked round the corner of the church and shrank out of sight. Peering around, she watched as the blank-faced driver heaved Annie's box up into the back of the carriage and held the door for her. Holding her drab blue skirts clear of the muck of the streets, Annie ducked inside the carriage and the driver slammed the door shut. As he jumped back up onto his seat at the front, Lydia edged slowly back to the main street and craned her neck to look in the carriage window at her sister as the horse started to move away. White-faced, Annie looked back at her and gingerly raised a hand. Brushing the dampness of the morning fog from her skirt, Lydia set off back to the house, keeping her eyes on the trailing hem of her dress.

She was quiet for the rest of the morning, and the other women in the house were particularly kind to her. Mary enveloped her in a huge hug the moment she walked in, and Daisy—who was looking very pale this morning, even before she'd had a chance to powder—ran a chilly hand down Lydia's paint-free face and tutted sympathetically. Despite the sisters' argument earlier in the week, even Kathleen did not seem as relieved to be rid of Annie as Lydia had expected her to be.

"Have a drink," she said, pouring a generous measure of brandy into a glass. "She was a prissy little brat, but I know this ain't easy for you."

Lydia shook her head and took a belt of the brandy. "No. And I know it's silly, really—all we did was quarrel, most of the time."

"Let's get you dressed up a bit," Mary said, combing her fingers through Lydia's ribbonless brown locks. "Your

Mr. Shadwell'll be here soon, and you'll feel better when you look less like a servant yourself."

When Lydia saw herself in the mirror, dolled up for Henry's pictures, she had to smile. She could hardly have looked less like the girl who had helped Annabel carry her trunk to meet her carriage. It was surprising how she could still look quite innocent when she tried. She pinned the crown brooch to her skirt, leaving a little strip of petticoat frothing out underneath it, and reached for the pots of paint on her dressing-table. She powdered her face, covering the pink flush that still hung around her eyes from lack of sleep and the yellowish remains of the bruise from when Kathleen had knocked her head against her sister's.

"Lydia?" Kathleen's voice drifted up the stairs. "Mr. Shadwell is here to collect you."

Down in the hallway, Mary and Daisy were in shawls and boots, ready to go out. Lydia's mouth fell open just the tiniest amount at her first thought, which was that Henry had decided that Lydia would not be sufficient after all, and wanted all three girls in front of his camera. It wouldn't be the first time a man had requested two or more of the girls at once. A landowner had once paid the house's bills for a week in exchange for a night with all three girls. Mary had taught him to use her whip on Lydia and Daisy, who both had backs striped like tabby cats for a fortnight.

"We'll walk you as far as the Bull," Mary said cheerily. Daisy, shivering even before the door had been opened, huddled further into her shawl.

"Be kind to her," Mary added, addressing Henry, who raised a quizzical eyebrow. "Her sister moved out."

"Of course," Henry said, eyeing Lydia. She looked back at him from under her lashes.

"Well, I haven't had the chance to get a drink yet this morning," Henry said. "What say the four of us stop at the Old Bull before we go on to my studio? That might lift your spirits a little."

Lydia blinked in surprise. "Ah . . . yes," she managed to say. "Yes, that would be fine."

The walk to the Bull was not long, but the biting November winds—the coldest Lydia could remember for years—made it seem unending. Daisy's face remained pale and drawn despite the cold, and she did not join in the casual conversation that passed between the others.

"Out picking a few up?" Lydia asked finally.

Mary slid her a tiny smile. "That's what I told Kathleen, but I said I'd meet Matty."

Lydia laughed. Matty Walsh was a local lad, a coiner as skilled at dodging the law as he was at passing fake money. His choirboy looks probably helped, but Lydia couldn't understand Mary's infatuation with him—to her, Matty looked like he was barely out of short trousers.

"Oi, Daisy!" Mary called across to their white and shivering friend. "Are you all right?"

Daisy didn't seem to hear her at first, but eventually she blinked and stirred herself.

"Oh . . . yes. Yes, I'm fine."

Lydia looked hard at Daisy, but the girl was staring blankly into the road again.

When she looked back at Henry, she noticed that he was watching Daisy intently, too.


The Bull was starting to fill up when they arrived, and Mary and Daisy took a table in the corner while Lydia and Henry went to the bar for drinks. As Henry ordered a whisky, Lydia looked out of the corner of her eye to the doorway, where Matty was just walking in. He glanced around the taproom for a fraction of a moment before raising a hand in greeting to Mary and sauntering towards her, slowing down only slightly to drop a pouch from his sleeve onto a table where a trio of men sat. By the time Lydia and Henry had made their way to the table, Mary and Matty were snuggled together in the corner. Daisy, who had been sitting closest to the fire, now looked red and sweaty, and she yanked her shawl from her shoulders and fanned herself with her spare hand.

"Daisy, are sure you're all right?" Lydia asked, pressing the back of her hand to her friend's damp forehead. "You've been like a block of ice all morning, and now you're burning up."

"I said I was fine."

"But Daisy—"

"I'm fine!" Daisy snapped. Before Lydia could reply, Henry looked over his shoulder and waved.

"Thomas!" Henry beckoned his fellow surgeon over, but as Thomas caught sight of the three girls, he slipped away into the clusters of people milling around in the taproom. Henry frowned.

"You keep running high and low temperatures?" he asked Daisy, suddenly alert. Lydia blinked; she didn't think he had been listening.

"Yes." Daisy stretched out the fingers of both her hands, wincing as if at some pain in the little joints. Henry nodded, and when he spoke again, his tone was hesitant.

"Then I'm afraid I must ask you: are you producing any . . . *abnormal fluids*, or having trouble making water?"

"Oh, lovely," Mary said, and Matty set his pint down on the table.

"Bloody surgeons," he grumbled. "Ghouls to a man."

Henry ignored him, and Lydia found that she was

watching Daisy as keenly as he was. Daisy drew a deep breath. She shivered, although her hair still clung limply to her sweaty forehead.

"It can't be the pox, though, can it?"

"I don't think it's that, no." Henry lowered his voice. "I think you may have come down with a case of gonorrhoea—you probably know it better as the clap," he added, looking at the bemused expressions on the girls' faces. "I hate to say it, but Thomas hadn't been himself for a few days before we first met the three of you. I saw him with a bottle of silver nitrate. I assumed it was for a patient." Henry frowned.

"Silver whatsit?" Lydia asked.

"Silver nitrate. It's one of the treatments for gonorrhoea—not one I'd favour, mind. It must have been for himself."

"But I can't have the clap!" Daisy squeaked. Glancing around to make sure that no one had heard, Lydia flapped a hand to shush her.

"How am I supposed to earn?" Daisy protested. "At least your mate Thomas can go on working!"

Mary told Matty to go and get the next round in. He made a show of grumbling, but offset it with a wink.

"Get a stout for her," Henry said, gesturing to Daisy as the coiner got to his feet, stacking the glasses in his arms. "It'll do her good."

"I'll need more than stout," Daisy protested. "I've got

to get rid of this thing! What's that silver stuff you were talking about?"

"It's silver nitrate, but I wouldn't if I were you," Henry said. "In my experience, that cure's usually worse than the disease: silver nitrate is an unpleasant substance, and it won't do more than suppress some of the symptoms anyway. Look, the illness has to run its course. Between you and me, you'll never be completely rid of it. It will come back from time to time for the rest of your days, if you're sick or exhausted. Really, I should be advising you to find alternative employment."

"Fucking marvellous," the angelic-looking Daisy mumbled under her breath.

"But I get the feeling such a suggestion would fall on deaf ears, and as I say, it's not like having syph . . . the pox," Henry said. "The best you can do is take some rest until it passes and keep your strength up. If you feel hot, try to cool yourself down. If you're cold, wrap up warm. It'll subside."

"Are you sure silver nitrate wouldn't get it over with quicker?" Mary asked, as Matty returned with the drinks and set them down on the scarred wooden tabletop. "Kathleen won't chuck her out, but a couple of days not earning ain't ideal."

Henry shook his head and supped from his mug of ale. "Neither is a blackened pudenda."

"Pudenda?"

"Cunt," Lydia explained, and Henry looked at her.

"Have you been reading those papers in the parlour again?"

"Yes—Annie took all her books with her."

"Hold up," Daisy interrupted. "Blackened?"

"It's the silver nitrate," Henry said. "Stains anything it touches. And that's just if you're lucky. If the mixture's not quite right, it burns. A chap I studied with used it when he got clapped and he said it was like having his prick set ablaze."

Matty looked as if he might throw up into his ale, and Lydia couldn't help but laugh. Ten minutes with the well-spoken, immaculately dressed Henry, and he was swearing as well as any whore.

"Well, what if she washes in spirits or piss?" Mary asked.

"If she really must, but it won't change the time it takes for her to recover, I'm afraid. Anyway," Henry said, digging his watch from his waistcoat pocket and studying it, "drink up, Lydia, and we'll go on our way. I want to get to my studio before noon, while the light's still good." Turning to Daisy, he indicated the pint of stout in front of her. "Have a couple more of those, then get yourself home and rest. It's not as bad as all that; as I said, you don't have the pox. Now that *is* something to be afraid of—I've known people worry themselves into believing they had that when they didn't. No men until it's cleared—your abbess won't want it put about that her girls are diseased."

Daisy nodded. "Thank you," she said. Lydia watched and waited for Henry to request something in payment for his advice, but he said nothing. Pulling on his overcoat, he held the door for Lydia as they stepped out into the street.

Henry hailed a cab to take them to his studio—it was out of town, over towards the docks, he explained. They'd not get an omnibus to take them that far. As they rattled past what must have been the fourth or fifth gaggle of street girls Lydia had seen since they set off, a question suddenly occurred to her.

"Henry," she asked, testing out the sound of his name, which, she now realized, she'd never actually spoken aloud, "why don't you get street girls or dollymops to model for you? It'd cost less." She had picked up a good enough sense of business from Kathleen, and though the last thing she wanted was to be replaced, she knew she had to hear his reasons.

"Moth-eaten," Henry replied, and Lydia narrowed her eyes in confusion. "Streetwalkers," he explained. "They're shabby. Tatty clothes, tangled hair, almost all of them diseased or bruised—there are plenty of photographs of them out there, certainly, but it's like it is with your own trade: a neat, clean model is a good investment. Men pay more for a better class of picture. As for the dollymops, I wouldn't expect them to be willing to pose for pictures like these. They have their other jobs to think of, and I'm sure they wouldn't want to run the risk of their employers finding the pictures."

It wasn't the answer Lydia had been wanting, and she started to wonder if she'd learned anything in her year at Kathleen Tanner's introduction house.

"Besides," Henry was saying as the cab bumped over the cracked cobbles, "they're too thin. No breasts on them." He reached a hand out to Lydia and smoothed it down the bodice of her burgundy dress, as if to press away a crease. Lydia felt a tingling deep in the middle of her body, and she slipped a hand down Henry's trousers. Henry stiffened as soon as her fingertips brushed his organ, but with a suppressed groan, he shook his head.

"Not yet," he said. She couldn't recall ever hearing those words from a man's lips.

"The pictures are always better before I indulge."

Lydia smiled her charming smile—always effective, rarely meant—and looked up at him from under her lashes.

"Then this isn't all about business?" she teased.

"I do have a pulse. I don't believe there's an artist alive who could resist his nudes when his work was done."

"Does Kathleen know this?"

Henry winked. "It's not as if we'll be using her premises, and she is being more than adequately compensated for your modelling services. We finally agreed that she should receive some samples of my work as well as the money. Just think of it as something between ourselves. It'll give you a little extra pin money."

Henry and his fingers *and* payments that Kathleen wouldn't see a penny of. Lydia turned her head away and beamed at the streaky glass in the cab window.


Henry's studio turned out to be a large room leased from the owner of a ramshackle white building that looked like an old boarding-house, not at all dissimilar to the one Lydia and Annie had lived in with their mother, when Nell was still alive. The floorboards squeaked as they walked through the hall and up the stairs. From the rotting doors that lurched drunkenly off the corridors and landings came all manner of sounds: the hastening grunts of a man approaching the end of his paid time with a whore; the sound of breaking glass; irate voices increasing in volume as an argument started to turn nasty.

As Henry directed Lydia to the dead end of a corridor, a man with glassy eyes staggered from one of the rooms, pushing past Lydia as he teetered off towards the stairs. The cloying scent of opium—something that was only ever smelled on the callers at Kathleen Tanner's house, never the girls—drifted from his filthy clothes.

Lydia listened for the sound of him crashing down the steps, but somehow it never came.

"It's the door at the end," Henry said.

The neighbouring door was boarded up. Henry's was the only one in the building that was locked. Digging a bunch of keys from his pocket, he fumbled with the lock and threw the door open.

The room was white, or rather a faded off-white, the paint cracked and peeling. The heels of Lydia's boots echoed on the bare floorboards. A torn and tatty sheet hung at the window, pulled carelessly aside. In the corner sat three wooden crates and a makeshift tent of thick black cloth; almost as tall as a man, with two narrow wooden poles raising the cloth up into a triangular formation as it swept down towards the grubby floorboards. A sharp stink emerged from within, catching at the back of Lydia's throat. Pressing the cuff of her dress sleeve to her mouth and nose, she looked around. The rest of the room was laid out almost like a lady's chamber, with a small wrought-iron bed with a filigreed head and lace-trimmed white linen that looked barely touched. A large piece of deep red wallpaper, reminiscent of that in Kathleen's parlour, was pinned up behind the bed, disguising the shabby paintwork underneath. One of the lower corners was torn, and beginning to curl upwards. A bedside table with a vase of flowers, a dressing-table with a mirror and an assortment of empty pots and jars arranged around a jewellery box completed the picture.

Overlooking it all, standing as if on sentry duty, was a curious-looking wooden creation; a box on three knobbly legs with pleats of leather along its sides and a swag of the black tent material hanging down the back of its ugly head.

"Welcome to my workplace," Henry said.

# 4

Walking over to the dressing-table, Lydia dug around in the jewellery box and pulled out a string of pearls, biting down on one as Mary had once taught her to do. The pearls weren't real, but they looked well enough.

"This ain't where you live, is it?" she teased Henry. "You big girl."

Henry's responding snort couldn't really be called a laugh, but his expression was amiable enough.

"Do you see anywhere I could keep my clothes?" he asked. "Or eat, for that matter?"

Draping the cheap pearls around her neck, Lydia padded around the room, exploring. On the far wall, she could now see, was a curtain that hung over an empty doorway, and she moved towards it.

"*Not* in there!" The sharpness in Henry's tone startled her, and she let her arm go slack as his hand clamped around her wrist. From behind the curtain, a strange smell drifted; sickly and sticky like the opium, but without the drug's hypnotic sweetness. Something about it repelled her, and a rush of fear tossed her heart up into her throat and let it fall back down again.

"I'm sorry," Lydia said.

"No matter," Henry replied, leading her back towards the boudoir set-up, "but you must not go in there without my express permission. It's better that you should stay out of there. Now, let me show you what to do."

The bed and dressing-table and pots of cream were there solely as props for the photographs. While Henry burrowed under the black hood at the back of the camera, Lydia eyed the overspilling jewellery box and wondered if he would miss one or two things, but decided against taking anything. Finally, under cover of the hood, Henry beckoned Lydia with one hand.

"Start taking a few garments off," he instructed her as he fiddled around, polishing the camera's little glass eye with the cuff of his shirtsleeve. "Just down to your corset and your last petticoat."

Slowly, Lydia unbuttoned her burgundy dress and let it fall from her shoulders. She looked across to Henry, but he wasn't paying attention. He kept ducking under the camera cloth, before ducking back out again and furrowing his brow thoughtfully as he examined the layout of the furniture and attempted to pin down the curling corner of the wallpaper. Pulling the bodice of her dress away, Lydia let the deep red material fall into a spreading puddle at her feet, and began to loosen her top petticoats.

"Are you sure you wouldn't rather I wore this one?" she asked, gesturing to the uppermost petticoat, which frothed with layers of flouncing lace and air-filled ruffles. "It's much prettier than my under-petticoat. That one's just plain; no lace or nothing."

"Quite sure," Henry said, walking over to the dressing-table to move a few of the pots and jars around. "The men who buy these pictures aren't fashion enthusiasts; they're buying them to see you. Your under-petticoat," he added, finally turning to look at Lydia, who had obediently undressed as requested, "is translucent. In the right light, the shape of your legs will show through."

To Lydia's great satisfaction, Henry's gaze rested on the thin fabric of her under-petticoat as it clung to her thighs, and as she trod on the heel of each boot in turn and kicked them off, it didn't move.

"Anything else?" she asked, her voice deliberately light and disinterested.

"Yes." With a couple of strides, Henry stood in front of Lydia and reached a hand around her back, tugging on her corset laces. His hands moved around to the front and Lydia held very still as he tugged at the stiff fabric, his fingers brushing lightly against her as he worked them behind the strips of whalebone. Slotting two fingers down the front of her corset, he adjusted the garment ever so slightly, so that an inviting shadow drew the eye down into the cleft between her breasts. Lydia felt the hot rush of victory as she noticed the bulge in the front of Henry's trousers. Tripping lightly across the floorboards in stock-inged feet, she pretended not to notice his rising desires, just as he had ignorèd hers. She would have all of his attention soon enough.

Never before had she been asked to hold so still. Once she was posed to Henry's satisfaction—reaching across the dressing-table as if to pick up a hairbrush; looking distractedly over her shoulder as if she had heard a sound in the street below; kneeling as if at prayer, her breasts spilling out of her corset—she was not to move a muscle until he told her to. Peering slyly under her lashes, she watched the blank eye of the camera as it stared at her. As time passed and Henry asked her, in an increasingly husky voice, to shed a little more of her clothing, Lydia loosened her laces, unhooked the top of her corset and stretched like a cat, allowing her breasts to slip free of the layer of stiff bone. The winter chill pinched her nipples and she turned so that Henry and the camera could admire her in profile.

As Lydia's underclothes fell away, Henry spoke less and less, and when she finally shed her corset altogether, it was without a single word from him. The tip of Henry's finger just below her shoulder startled her, and he trailed it down a tender pink streak left by her corset. Lydia dropped her petticoat from her hips, and strolled to the dirty window in her favourite damson drawers and her stockings. Resting her hands on the sill, she looked down into the filthy cobbled street below, where women in shabby old rags jostled each other to snatch the better wares from the street-sellers, and flea-bitten dogs locked jaws and snarled as they rolled around fighting. Nobody looked up to the window.

Leaning coltishly on one hip, Lydia gazed out at the skyline as if she were a hundred miles away in thought. In truth, she breathed quietly and listened to every tiny sound in the room behind her: the rattling of plates, the whispering rasp of Henry's head emerging from underneath the camera's hood, the chink of metal as he covered the camera's glass eye with a copper disc, and the soft fall of his feet coming closer and closer. She did not move, not even when he was so close she could feel the heat of his breath on the back of her neck.

He had her around the waist in an instant, and his body pushed against hers. He fumbled with her drawers, tugging them down while she wriggled her hips to help him free her. Slowly, she turned her head, pressing her cheek against the glass of the window and revelling in the silent contrast of the coldness on her face and breasts and the heat of Henry's body against hers. She shifted slightly—just a little, just enough for him to get to her—and bent a little further over the sill. Over her shoulder, she could see him unbuttoning his trousers, and she closed her eyes so that she would not know exactly when to expect it.

She was throbbing with an ache that she had only known when Henry had last touched her, and when, late at night, she had slid her own fingers down beneath the bedsheets, imagining that they were his. Then Henry pushed into her, and Lydia wriggled back against him.

He wrapped one arm around her waist to hold her to him, and trailed his free hand down. Even without that magical touch, she had been desperate for him to fuck her, but now that he was gently tracing his fingers up and down against her while he thrust into her, she felt the whole world melt away. Each breath shuddered from her as if it were her last.

When Henry withdrew, the scents of their bodies

mingled in the air and Lydia drew a deep, discreet breath.
She was used to ignoring the smell of her customers, but
this was different. Less the smell of a spent man, more
herself and Henry combined.

"So can I see my pictures, then?" she asked Henry, who
had tucked himself away and now stood inside the little
black tent with his back to Lydia.

"Oh, they won't be ready for some hours. They need
to be developed and printed first." He held up one of the
bottles, and Lydia nodded and adopted her expression
of interest.

"I use silver nitrate to develop these pictures, by the
way. Here."

As she walked across to where Henry stood with a
handful of papers clutched in one hand, Lydia pulled a
blanket from the bed and wrapped it around her naked
shoulders. She was shivering a little now that the frenzy
had subsided, and her clothes would take some time to
get back into.

"I took these when I first bought the camera," he said,
pressing a picture of a thin girl, stripped to the waist, into
Lydia's hands. The illustrations in the papers Kathleen
kept in the parlour were all lithographs, and she had
never really seen a picture like this before. The girl in
this picture was real; her image captured in shades of

black, white and grey: the girl's skin was white, while her eyes were black and the faint shadows under her ribs were streaked with a delicate grey.

"Not my best work, of course. I was just starting out, and I was still using cheap prostitutes then, as you can see. This is one I did a few months back."

The next photograph was of a dark-haired girl like Lydia, obviously better kept than the last. She stood facing forward, completely nude, with her arms stretched out above her and her chin turned up, contemplating the ceiling as Lydia had seen stone angels contemplate the sky above them in graveyards. The light from the window seemed to flow like water down between the girl's breasts, over the soft curve of her belly and down to the dark mask between her rounded thighs. Lydia shifted slightly.

"We didn't take any like this," she commented. "Without any clothes at all, I mean."

"We will," Henry said, "but the light was fading; it looks as if it's going to rain. Besides," he added with a smirk, "I got distracted."

Lydia laughed. "So will I be all white and grey, too?"

"Yes," Henry replied. "We do not yet have a way to capture colour well. It is possible to pay someone to add colour to a picture, but far too expensive an endeavour for a project like mine. Still, things are improving all the time—look at this old one."

She squinted at the pale, scratchy picture Henry

handed to her. The girl—or rather, woman—was a little older than Lydia. She stared blankly back as if she didn't care in the least that Henry was now disparaging her image.

"How old?" Lydia asked.

"About twenty years or so."

Lydia pondered on this for a while, before another thought came to her.

"So," she said, reaching out to hold the picture between thumb and forefinger, "the girl in this will be . . . how old now? Forty?"

"Somewhere between thirty-five and forty, I should guess," Henry answered. He had gone back to fiddling with the strange-smelling bottles in the tent, and Lydia stared at the image in her hand.

There was not a chance that the woman would still look like she did in this photograph. Even in the faded, marked old picture, Lydia could see that her skin was smooth and soft, her hair dark with colour, and the curves of her body round and inviting. All would have started to wither by now if she was in her fortieth year or more, especially given that she was a prostitute—a whore's life wasn't easy.

Lydia, Mary, Daisy, every whore who walked the streets or lay back in an introduction house, all of them had only a few short years before they would start to wilt, as the model in this old picture must surely be wilting now. Who would pay them then?

She thought of Kathleen: a good-looking woman, certainly, but no girl—not one that men would pay to act as if they were still handsome young swains with an irresistible charm. Kathleen must have realized what would happen: the men dwindling as the years passed, losing her place in the introduction house to a young girl who would bring them back to the door, finally reduced to walking the streets outside the pubs at chucking-out time in the hope of making a few pennies from men who were too drunk to notice or care that this was no ripe-bodied young woman. Then there were the bugs a girl could pick up along the way, and while Kathleen swore by olive oil as a precaution, no girl in the trade could expect it to keep her safe indefinitely. All you could hope for was a little more time.

"Right," Henry said, emerging from the tent, his hands stained a tea-like brown, "I'll take you back now."

Lydia was quiet as the cab rattled across the uneven roads around the River Ribble. Gazing out of the window at the town being paraded past her, she watched the straggly gangs of small, skinny children as they paddled ankle-deep in the muddy water of the riverbanks. The mudlarks clawed through the dirt and muck, searching for sellable scraps before the tide came in. Once, Lydia had seen a mudlark shriek in pain as he paddled ankle-deep in the

Ribble, before bending down and beaming as he discovered that it was a copper nail he had trodden on, and one
in good enough nick to sell, at that.

Outside the introduction house she hopped out of the
cab, with Henry stepping down after her. He handed
the driver an extra coin and asked him to wait outside.
The man leered down at Lydia. She was used to that: there
surely wasn't a driver in town who hadn't dropped a
man off outside Kathleen's house and been asked to wait
outside. As she turned and walked up to the house she
realized that she was following Henry, as if she were
here on his invitation. He rang the doorbell, and as they
waited, rummaged through his case and pulled out a sheaf
of papers.

To Lydia's surprise it wasn't Kathleen that came to
the door but Mary, and she was in a hell of a state. Barg-
ing Henry out of the way and nearly sending his papers
flying, Mary grabbed Lydia by the shoulders and shook
her. The Irish girl was stronger than she looked.

"Mary, what's the matter?"

At that moment, Kathleen appeared at Mary's elbow.
With a quick glance out into the street, she grabbed her
two girls by their dresses and pulled them inside. In the
hall, Lydia looked to Mary for an answer, but her friend's

lip had started to tremble and she looked near to tears. Kathleen scrutinized Henry for a split second—only one who knew her could have seen her brief failure to place his face—before beckoning to him.

"You'd best come in, Mr. Shadwell," she said grimly.

The parlour was empty, and Kathleen swept them all in with a practised gesture. Baffled, Henry stood holding out his handful of papers to the abbess. It was the first time Lydia had seen him look even slightly ill at ease in his surroundings. Kathleen took the papers from him with a distracted glance and tossed them onto the coffee table, where they landed with a soft thud and fanned out, displaying pages of closely-printed text, lithographs of chorus girls with their skirts hitched up to their knees, and even a few of the greyish photographs of bare-breasted whores with indecipherable expressions.

"Tell them," Kathleen said to the trembling Mary.

Mary caught her breath. "They've taken Daisy. The Society must've tipped the law off. They showed up in the Bull and spotted us before I could sneak out the side door. You know how sick she were looking."

"And they saw it straight away." Henry's voice was smooth and confident, his poise returned.

"Yes," Mary whispered helplessly. "I managed to get away in all the fuss, but Daisy . . . well, you know she weren't herself."

Lydia looked at Mary, and in her friend's fear-blackened

eyes she could see her own anxious expression. The
Society—the local Society for the Prevention of Vice—
crept through the town's underbelly like a sewer rat, sniffing out indulgence and debauchery with an unnervingly
keen hunger, and feeding information to the police, who
sent out men in plain clothes to investigate. None of the
prostitutes they took on suspicion of spreading disease
saw them coming.

Lydia and Mary held onto each other's dress sleeves
like frightened children, and even Kathleen looked as
if she had lost a close relative. Of course, Lydia didn't
know how much of the abbess's concern was for the
reputation of her house.

"Bloody Society," Kathleen hissed. "I've never known
a fuss like it, and I've been in the trade since I were a lass
myself."

"She'll be at the hospital," Henry said confidently.
"They'll examine her on the venereal ward there. Unfor-
tunately I cannot say that they will find no disease. I
presume you have been told, Mrs. Tanner?"

Kathleen nodded quickly. "Is there any chance of them
releasing her? It's not as if she's poxed, is it?"

"The pox would be a bigger problem, but the clap is
hardly going to be overlooked. If she was continuing to
work, she'd still pass it on, and between the four of us, I
believe that may be a sore point, let us say, with many of
the men in the Society. In any case, if Daisy resists deten-
tion in a locked ward, they'll simply try her case before

a magistrate. And if it comes to that, she won't merely have to prove she isn't a prostitute; she'll have to prove she's a virgin."

Kathleen opened her mouth to speak, but Henry interrupted her.

"And they won't fall for any of your tricks with menstrual fluid or pig's blood—they've seen it all before."

"Well, what if you go to the hospital?" Lydia piped up. "They'll drag any of us in there as likely as look at us, yes, but not you. Can't you go and check on Daisy? Get them to let her go, even?"

"Lydia!" Kathleen had remembered herself. "You can't make demands of Mr. Shadwell, you know that."

Privately, Lydia was surprised at herself, too.

"Let her be, Mrs. Tanner, I'd be more than happy to offer what help I can," Henry said. "I sincerely doubt that I can make a case for her release, but I shall certainly try to get some more information for you."

"I'm coming with you," Lydia said.

"Very well, but you must stay in the cab," Henry said. "They must not see you."

# 5

It was raining heavily by the time the cab pulled up outside the hospital. The driver hopped down to open the door for Henry and insisted that Lydia get out too. She eyed the pouring clouds and the driver's dripping cap and sodden clothes with dread.

Henry offered to pay him to wait, but the cab driver was having none of it, and Lydia stepped down, grumbling, onto the wet path outside.

"What now?" she asked, as the cab rattled away.

"Well, you can't come into the hospital. Make sure you keep out of sight."

Lydia nodded. A drop of rain slid down her forehead and off the tip of her nose.

"Here," Henry said, draping his overcoat around her shoulders, "you'll get chilled." Before she could thank him, he strode off towards the looming face of the hospital, and she was left pulling the thick black wool of his coat around herself, snuffling at the scent that still lingered in the collar. Somewhere a door banged, and she backed into the shelter of a pair of oak trees, drew the black coat around her red dress, and tried for the first time in a long time to be inconspicuous.

As the wind whipped the branches of the trees, the raindrops fell heavier and heavier, plastering her hair to her head and face. She looked over to the black-painted door that Henry had disappeared through. A high sandstone arch loomed over it, and above that, row upon row of windows with curtains drawn. A clap of thunder rumbled overhead, and Lydia hoisted Henry's coat up over her head and peered from underneath it as she heard the low sound of voices coming closer. Two men; neither of them Henry. She slipped behind the thick trunk of one of the oaks, wishing that the coat were long enough to cover her skirts, and watched them walk past her and down the path towards the hospital. She wondered if one of the men had been the one to examine Daisy. Slowly, she stepped back around the tree and craned her neck for any sign of Henry.

A hand clapped onto her shoulder, muffled by the thick wool of Henry's overcoat. Startled, Lydia jumped and spun around, but before she could shriek, Henry's hand flew to her mouth, and she heaved a ragged sigh of relief.

"Quiet," Henry whispered. She nodded, mute, and he drew his hand away.

"Come on," he said, "we'll talk once we're inside a cab."

Finding an unoccupied cab in such weather was not easy, and they were soaked to the skin by the time Henry flagged one down. As they bundled into the back, Lydia realized that she still had his overcoat around her shoulders, and a dense wet wool smell was coming from Henry's jacket.

"Well, I can see you don't have her with you," she started.

"No," he said, sweeping rainwater off his leather case with the back of his hand, "but that was to be expected, as I said."

Lydia murmured a reluctant agreement and waited for him to go on.

"Daisy was taken up this afternoon because the arresting constable thought she looked ill," Henry said. "She will have undergone the procedure all the girls go through in these circumstances."

A shadow flitted over Lydia's face, and she looked at Henry, her head tilted to one side. She didn't believe for one moment that the interests of the men who carried out these "examinations" were solely scientific.

"I didn't get to *see* Daisy, never mind speak to her. I

doubt very much that they would have told me anything if I hadn't been a surgeon." He frowned. "I had to spin them a tale about her being a distant cousin of someone working for a patient of mine. I doubt they believed it, but it encouraged them to tell me a little."

"Thank you," Lydia said. She looked over at Henry; he was thoroughly drenched, his mahogany hair darkened by the rain and hanging in rats' tails across his forehead. His coat was open and she could see through the sodden white linen of his shirt to the warm pink of his chest, speckled with dark hairs. She blinked, as if to break the strange spell, and pulled his coat from her shoulders. He took it from her, his fingers brushing hers.

"They diagnosed gonorrhoea, of course," he said, clearing his throat and shifting slightly in his seat. "They're holding her for six months . . . It could have been worse," he added as Lydia's mouth fell open in shock. "If she had been syphilitic it would have been nine. I should imagine they'll just keep her on the ward here rather than transport her to one of the special hospitals in Manchester or Liverpool. When she comes out she should be able to get back to your house without too much trouble."

"Can we visit her?" Lydia asked. "If we washed off our paint and wore something dowdy, like? Or send her a gift, some food, maybe?"

Henry shook his head. "I can't go back there, either—I can't risk my professional reputation." Seeing Lydia's raised eyebrow, he gave her a crooked smile. "All you can do is wait for her release, my dear, and hope that her detainment is . . . uneventful."

Mary paled when Henry repeated his findings back at the introduction house, while Kathleen stood in silence, except to thank Henry for checking on Daisy. Faced with three mute women, Henry fidgeted with his case and finally announced that he had an appointment on the other side of town.

"I'll come by tomorrow afternoon to collect Lydia— shall we say three o'clock?" he asked Kathleen.

"Yes, that will be perfectly fine, thank you, Mr. Shadwell."

"Henry."

"As you like, sir."

Mary slipped out after supper, ostensibly to drum up trade in the Bull and quell any rumours about the health of Kathleen Tanner's girls.

"I don't know how you can face it tonight," Lydia said. "I just want to hide under the covers and let them all go to hell. They can abuse themselves if they need to spend so badly." Even as she said it, she knew that if a man came knocking, he'd end up in her room. Lord only knew, few men would have got as far as the top of the stairs if her feelings were all there was to the matter.

Mary glanced over her shoulder, crept into the room and closed the door behind her.

"Listen," she whispered, sitting on the rumpled bed beside Lydia. "I'm meeting Matty. After they took Daisy he told me to meet him at six so he knew I was safe. I'll unpin my skirts once I get there. I just need to spend some time with my lad." Her cheeks had taken on a subtle pink glow.

"You ain't going soft on him, are you?" Lydia asked.

Mary smiled shyly, and in that moment Lydia could see the sweet girl she had been: barely recognizable as the cruelly beautiful harridan who flogged and tormented men for their pleasure.

"I think I love him, Lydia."

Lydia clucked her tongue sympathetically. "Oh come on now, Mary. That's nought but trouble for girls like us, you've told me often enough."

"Listen to you!" Mary crowed. "As if you don't go all black-eyed for that Mr. Shadwell and hang on his every word. It's not like you're going to end up as a surgeon's wife, is it?"

Lydia bristled. "I never said I wanted to be, did I?" she snapped. "Wives don't have it much better than us. Men feed them and clothe them in exchange for having all their demands satisfied—the only difference is that wives never get to see and hold money that's theirs alone. And at least we don't have to birth a baby every year. I don't want to be Henry's wife, or anyone else's, thank you." Mary smiled a brittle smile of disbelief, and Lydia tossed her head, annoyed. "You'll be late," she said. "Matty will think the Society took up two whores rather than just the one."

She would have stayed in her room all night, but Kathleen came up after an hour or so and told her that she'd best be down in the parlour, since Mary was out fishing. Lydia nodded, as if it were true, but sitting alone in the parlour, flipping through the papers Henry had left, her thoughts drifted to Annie and Daisy, both of whom had disappeared from her life so completely and so quickly. She remembered her first days in Kathleen's house, when Daisy had taken her to buy her new clothes, paid for with her first earnings. It had been Daisy who, to Lydia's great relief, had swept her past the market stalls hawking the shapeless brown and grey smocks she had been used to, and towards the ready-made gowns sold by seamstresses who could afford neither a shop of their own nor to throw the likes of Kathleen's girls away from their door.

Daisy had helped her pick out the first underclothes she had ever owned—apart from her tatty linen shifts—

and back at the house, she and Mary had taught Lydia how to arrange her stockings and camisole, before helping her into her corset, which Mary laced up mercilessly each morning until she learned to do it herself. Between them, the girls had taught Lydia the words and actions that would revive a limp prick, or hurry along a man who was taking up too much of her time. Whatever anybody else might say, those lessons had stood her in richer stead than peddling laces on the street.

She turned the page of the periodical in her hands and looked into the eyes of a nude woman. She thought again of the woman in Henry's faded picture, whose face would now be lined and her body slowly crumpling like the skin of overripe fruit.

The jangling doorbell roused her from her thoughts, and she heaved a resentful sigh as she heard Kathleen's voice in conversation with rumbling, male tones. Kathleen showed the man in and indicated Lydia, allowing the man—plain-faced, plainly dressed, dull of voice—to decide whether or not he wanted her. He did. They always did.

Forty minutes later, Lydia was lying flat on her belly on the bed, with her skirts pulled up around her waist, the man forcing his breath out with each thrust, as if he were learning difficult dance steps. He'd been at this for a while now, and Lydia had to admit to herself that she was surprised. She clenched tightly and buried her face in the pillow, relieved that at least he didn't want her on her back, where she'd have to look him in the face. Instead she turned and looked at his hand planted on the pillow beside her head. Yes, he was wearing a wedding ring (as did many of the married men who could afford the prices in Kathleen's house), and it didn't look new.

"Oh," she tutted, "you're married. What a pity." That always either finished them or scared them away, and for added effect she brushed the smooth gold of the wedding band with her fingers.

It worked. A croak, a final jolt, and Lydia chuckled silently into her pillow, before sighing as if in release.


She closed the door of her room behind him, and pulled off her clothes as soon as she heard his footsteps on the stairs. The stale tobacco smell of his breath lingered on the back of her dress, and when she moved, the layers of her petticoats rustled with a clinging, sweaty odour. She stripped down to her under-petticoat and corset, before reaching around and wrestling with her laces. Then she kicked off her damp drawers and poked them away with her toes.

Her paint felt sticky on her face. Usually she couldn't be frigged removing it—as evidenced by her pillow, which was frequently smeared with pinks and reds—but tonight it seemed to be suffocating her, so she sat down in front of her dressing-table and set about looking in the drawers for the pot of cold cream Kathleen had given her. She found it—a heavy brown glass jar with a glass stopper—and set it on the table in front of her. Just as she was about to close the drawer, something caught her eye.

Two books—one thick and bound in leather, the other thin and paper-covered, with Annabel's name neatly handwritten on the front. Lydia picked the books up and studied them more closely. The smaller volume was one of Annie's old exercise books. Flicking through the pages, she recognized the lines of increasingly well-formed letters that Annie had made as she learned to write; the same letters that Lydia had copied onto the backs of old correspondence and bills when her sister had set her mind to passing on her skill. Annie must have left these for her on purpose. She picked up the heavy, leather-bound book and examined it more closely. The title was stamped in gold on the grainy black leather: HOLY BIBLE. She knew this book, too. It was the one Annie had let her use to practise her reading and writing.

Setting the Bible down on the tabletop, Lydia pulled the stopper from the jar of cold cream and scooped out a palmful. Smoothing the cream into her skin, she closed her eyes, relishing the soft, cool strokes. Opening her eyes, she looked into the mirror at the strange, awkward sight of her clean face. She felt freer, but her skin seemed mottled, and when she moved closer to the glass every little flaw seemed enormous.

She stood and padded, barefoot, to the window and drew the curtain back so that she could look down into the pitch-black street below. Still no sign of Mary, and it was past chucking-out time by now. She must be with Matty somewhere. Something in Lydia bristled at the thought. Sighing, she let the curtain fall back and returned to the dressing-table. Her under-petticoat swished as she moved, tickling the backs of her legs. Sitting down, she jammed her finger between the pages of the Bible, letting it fall open where it would. Her hazelnut eyes skimmed the tiny, closely printed text.

"I speak after the manner of men because of the infirmity of your flesh . . ."

Lydia knew that this was a special book, an important one for any Christian, so she'd been all the more surprised when she'd read it—page after page of plummy-toned riddles and bedtime stories for children.

"For the wages of sin is death . . ."

She slammed the book shut and flipped back to the beginning, to the first story she'd read without Annie's help; the one in the garden of Eden where Eve ate the apple and suddenly she and Adam felt the need to cover their bodies with leaves. That bit always made Lydia smile—no old age, sickness or death, just a silly slut who thought a leaf over her cunt would stop a man from seeking it out.

The next morning, she left Mary to sit in the parlour in case of visitors and headed into town. Kathleen had given her a list of things for the house, and by the time Lydia had dragged herself up Fishergate to the iron-monger's her arm ached under the weight of the basket, laden with bread and meat and oil and bottles of whisky and port for the parlour. She had considered going to a proper stationer to buy the things she needed, but King's Ironmonger's sold just about everything, and a good deal cheaper, too. A little brass bell rang as she entered.

Miss King, the shop owner, gaunt and dowdy in the black she always seemed to wear, looked across at Lydia from behind the counter, where she stood wrapping candles for a small woman in quality clothes, whose husband waited beside her. A tiny, fair-haired girl ran around and around the shop, weaving in and out of the shelves and coming perilously close to knocking their wares off onto the floor. Both Miss King and the waiting woman checked when they saw Lydia, their gazes raking her, from her exposed flash of petticoats up. The little woman's hand tightened on the arm of the distinguished man beside her.

"I need some paper and a pen and some ink," Lydia said smoothly, as if harlots bought writing supplies every day. "Whichever sell best will be fine." At that moment, the giddy child ran into the back of her legs.

The other customer raised a thin, pale eyebrow, and reached out to take her daughter by the hand, drawing her away from Lydia. "Then you can wait your turn."

"Suit yourself." Lydia made a show of fluttering her eyelashes at the woman's husband, who had been watching the scene with an expression of quiet amusement. His wife seemed less entertained, and bustled her family out of the shop as soon as her candles were parcelled up and paid for.

Miss King regarded Lydia with a filthy look before turning to the shelves, pulling a pen from a jar and testing its nib with her fingertip, and scooping a little bottle of black ink into the crook of her arm. She glanced at Lydia, but did not speak, even as she proffered two different parcels of writing paper for her to choose from. Equally silent, Lydia nodded towards the larger packet.

She had every intention of going straight back to the house to practise, but she had barely taken more than a dozen steps back up Fishergate when she heard the hollow clop of a horse's hooves behind her, slowing and stopping. The driver beckoned to her and, with a stab of irritation, Lydia turned with a sweet smile and her head held high. She cleared her throat.

"Just a pound to a handsome man like yourself," she said.

The clerk regarded her with a piscine, eye-bulging expression.

"Ah . . . yes," he said, jerking to life and fumbling in his coat pocket as she climbed into the carriage.

# 6

Afterwards, he dropped her off in Winckley Square, and Lydia decided to walk through the square's public gardens to raise her spirits before she had to return to Kathleen's. Stepping down from the carriage and through the gates of the gardens, Lydia hoisted the basket into the crook of her elbow and wound her way along the crunchy path. The gardens looked deserted, and the grass, cut back for winter, gave off only a ghost of its sweet perfume. A gust of wind chilled Lydia, and she pulled her shawl closer around herself. The familiar clamminess on her thighs was making her under-petticoat feel sticky, and the gauzy fabric itched. She huffed impatiently, and tossed her head. As she did so, she caught sight of a familiar figure in front of her. Squinting against the harsh winter morning light, she hooded her eyes with her hand to keep the sun out of them.

"Annie!"

The navy-clad girl on the path ahead of her jumped, and wheeled around nervously. Lydia nipped her lower lip as she realized why: two identical small girls in immaculate dresses with far too many bows were running around in the grass a few feet from her sister. The Hollingworth girls. Guilt twisted Lydia's guts at the thought of exposing Annie as a prostitute's sister in her first week with her new employer. But Annabel actually seemed glad to see her. With a quick glance at the twins, she beckoned Lydia, who strolled towards her as if she had all the time in the world.

"It's all right," Annie said, with another glance at the girls. "Lavinia! Lilia! Stay where I can see you, now." The children were rummaging through a pile of fallen leaves, collecting acorns. "It's just us. But turn your back."

Of course. With her back turned, Annie's charges would not be able to see the signs that set Lydia apart from other women—her painted face, her tucked-up skirts. The two Ketch girls turned and spoke in low voices, Annie glancing over her shoulder every now and then to keep watch on the children. Her nose wrinkled slightly and Lydia realized that Annie must be able to smell the clerk on her.

"How are you keeping?" Lydia asked, "Kathleen's

isn't the same without you, you know." She was surprised to see Annie smile softly, as if in remembrance of a cherished childhood home, rather than the den of iniquity she had been so embarrassed to live in and so eager to leave. "I expect you've not had a chance to write to me yet, have you? You're probably very busy." After spending almost all her life so far with her sister, even a few days without hearing from her had been strange for Lydia. She waited for her sister to give her new address as she had promised, but in vain.

"No," Annie admitted. "I'm sorry. There's been so much happening, but every time I sat down to write you a letter . . ." she shrugged. "I never knew what to say. But how are you? How is everyone?"

Lydia was about to start rattling off an account of Daisy's illness and arrest, when she spied a twinkling teardrop on the edge of Annie's pale lashes.

"Well enough," she lied. "But what's this, Annie?" She reached up and brushed the tear from her sister's eye. "Two little girls can't be as much trouble as Mary, can they?" She tried a smile, but Annie's attempt at laughter caught in her throat and turned into a sob.

"Oh," Lydia soothed, putting her arms around Annie, despite what the children might say. "Annie, what's to do?"

Annabel shook her head violently and wiped her eyes on her gloves. Again she glanced back at the girls, but they were playing with sycamore seeds, watching them spin through the air. She opened her mouth, before closing it again with a sigh.

"Nothing," she said eventually. "I'm probably just being soft, I need to get used to things. This is a wonderful opportunity for a girl like me—I'm a governess! I shouldn't complain."

Lydia looked steadily at her. She knew Annie's sulks and tantrums, but this time her distress seemed very real.

"What is it, Annie? You can tell me."

"No, really." Annie shook her head vigorously. "You know me—I get maudlin sometimes. Nothing's wrong."

"Yes, I do know you, and that's how I know this is different. What is it, Annabel?"

Again Annie parted her lips and caught her breath, and Lydia leaned closer.

"Lydia . . . how are you?"

The absurdity of her question caused Lydia to snort involuntarily. "How am I? What does that have to do with anything? We're talking about you!"

Annabel shook her head firmly. "Just tell me how you're feeling, Lydia, please. Are you well enough? Happy? Please."

A sigh. "Yes, I'm fine." The spectre of Daisy flitted into her mind, but Lydia pushed it away, determined that she was not going to add to Annie's worries.

"Really? You know, it's only since I got my place with the Hollingworths that I realized how little I asked you about your own life."

Lydia smiled ruefully. "You didn't want to know, did you? You know most of what my life entails, Annie, and what you didn't know you'd not ask about." Annie's eyes lowered guiltily at that, and Lydia gently nudged her arm. "Come now, there's no need to get over-wrought. I don't blame you for not wanting to know—I wish I didn't, half the time. Don't upset yourself, Annie."

Annie nodded vigorously, palming tears from her wind-reddened cheeks. "Aye, all right. Still, I should have asked. You're my sister and you kept us both by doing . . . *those things* with all those men. I never did thank you."

Lydia shrugged. She wasn't sure what to say to that.

"But you *are* well enough, aren't you?" Annie repeated.

"I'm perfectly well, and as happy as most of us are, I reckon. Now will you tell me what the matter is?"

"Then you're not . . . ?" Annie tailed off. Childish voices made them both jump. The Hollingworth girls were running towards them with their aprons filled with leaves and conkers. Lydia turned her face away.

"Oh, look at your aprons!" Annie complained. Then, speaking to Lydia in an undertone, "I'll have to go." She led the girls towards the gate without a backward glance. Lydia almost called after her, but her sister's name died on the tip of her tongue as she stifled herself.

With her eyes on her feet, she trudged after Annabel and the twins, who had almost disappeared from sight. The gate squeaked on its hinges, and Lydia was left alone in the gardens.

Henry picked her up after lunch. Throughout the cab ride to the docks he talked excitedly about the success of Lydia's last batch of pictures and how well they had been selling. She realized now, for the first time, that he wasn't always cool and impassive. His dark eyes twinkled with a mischievous, self-satisfied light, and he broke into a broad smile that Lydia found as commanding as his usual detached expression. His enthusiasm was infectious, and by the time they were in his studio, she felt giddy and almost carefree.

It seemed success made him relax. He allowed his hands to linger on Lydia and his face to nuzzle her nape, while he gently pressed her into the poses he desired. Again she stood still, her arms and legs slowly growing heavier and aching under the strain, the camera's impassive glass eye watching her unblinking until Henry told her she could move and he changed the plate. With each pose, more of her clothing fell away, until finally she was kneeling in just her drawers and stockings. Emerging from the camera's black hood, Henry nodded.

"Good," he said, taking her hands and pulling her to

her feet. "Now, I was thinking perhaps today we should take some without any clothing whatsoever. Try to look as if you're not aware of the camera."

"Like my mind's somewhere else, you mean?"

Henry chuckled. "There speaks the voice of experience. You'll offend me at this rate."

Lydia didn't apologize, for she knew Henry's acerbic wit well enough by now. She laughed instead, and watched him as he disappeared once again into the little tent.

"So," she said, reaching down to tug at the foot of one of her stockings, "you're a surgeon who gives free advice to whores and visits them in hospital and takes pictures of them to sell. You have a studio with a room I'm not allowed to see, you like paying for women, and you like a drink in the afternoons." She whipped her other stocking off and laid them both next to her on the bedsheets, then smiled with forced casualness. "What do you do when you're being respectable, then?"

Henry smirked. "I heal the sick, try to prevent illness, and pretend I'm appalled by the number of young women on our streets, spreading disease. And I teach, of course." A shadow passed across his face, and he paused, considering. "Although I suppose that isn't a part of my respectable persona. It's not exactly something one can chat about at dinner parties."

"Then why put your paid work at risk?"

Henry looked at her. "For the same reason I 'give free

advice to whores,' because I believe in what I'm doing . . ."
His voice had lowered to a mutter and he ducked back
into the tent and clattered some of his bottles about.
"Most of the people in Preston simply cannot afford a
surgeon," he continued from the darkness. "It matters not
whether they have a mild fever or are on their deathbed;
they must do without."

Lydia nodded. "My ma never had anyone out to her
while she was dying." It seemed strange to refer to Nell
Ketch by that name again: though Lydia had thought of
Nell often since she'd been living in Kathleen's house,
she had hardly spoken of her. Whenever she thought of
her mother, she always thought of her as "Nell."

"Yes, exactly," Henry was saying as he emerged from
underneath the camera's hood, "and if the best they can
get is an apothecary or a barber, then the apothecaries
and barbers might as well know how to treat the more
common ailments properly. Some of their work is good,
of course—I wouldn't hesitate to recommend some of
their remedies—but too many die for want of a learned
opinion."

Lydia frowned. Henry's eyes were shining again.

"But surely you don't want every man in town who
owns a pestle and mortar or a bone-saw to become a
surgeon," she protested. "You won't eat!"

"All I do is impart a little anatomical knowledge to
men who wouldn't know what they were doing otherwise. I'm hardly creating competition—do you think

people who could afford me would be seen turning to a lesser man? My living is safe." He ducked back under the hood and peered through the camera.

"And perhaps," Henry's muffled voice said, "I can save a few lives this way that I wouldn't have saved otherwise. It's no bad thing." His face, when he reemerged, softened something in Lydia: his dark eyes looked anxious, as if he had said too much. She smiled gently.

"I understand," she said quietly.

Just as they were getting ready to take the last photographs while there was still enough light, there was a tap at the door. While Lydia buttoned her dress, Henry put his ear to the door. "Who is it?" he said.

Lydia couldn't make out the muffled reply, but Henry nodded and unlocked the door.

"Come in."

A rangy man with a swarthy complexion and unruly stubble entered the room. He looked around, but seemed to see straight through Lydia. Turning back to Henry, he held up a satchel.

"More already?"

The man grinned. "Yes. If you ever decide to dedicate your efforts to the sick, Shadwell, I'll be ruined."

Henry was over by the black tent, flicking through

the pictures that filled the crates just outside. "God forbid I ever do anything so foolish, hmm?"

"Amen."

"Will these suffice?" Henry walked back to the dark-featured man, holding aloft a thick pile of photographs. The stranger flicked through them.

"They should do."

Henry fed the photographs carefully into the open satchel, and the man buckled it closed. Then he turned back to Lydia. "I thought I recognized you. You're the new girl, aren't you?" He patted the satchel.

"Yes, Lydia's my new model," said Henry. "Lydia, this is John Fletcher. He sells some of my photographs."

Lydia nodded and smiled politely.

"I'm down Glovers Court," Fletcher explained. "I have a bookshop right below Stan Stoker's printworks, so I sell his papers and all. Get quite a bit of trade there, and I can hardly keep your pictures in. Just shows you people will pay more for quality. And right here in town, too! A word to the wise, though, Shadwell—I've been keeping my ear to the ground, and so should you."

"Society?" Henry asked casually, but Lydia was instantly alert. She caught herself taking little glances at the curtain hanging over the door to Henry's secret workshop, as if she were expecting plain-clothes constables to storm out and snatch her up.

"Yes, but it's different this time. The Society's obviously

got the law worked up about this sort of thing. I've actually had coppers coming in, and I know a bloke who's had his stock seized. Magistrate ordered it all destroyed."

Henry's expression changed in an instant. "They've been into your shop? And they didn't find anything?"

"No, but they've had better luck with other booksellers. I'm careful."

Henry frowned. "I doubt the others had them out on the shelves, Fletcher. Don't be too sure of yourself."

# 7

Mention of the Society spooked her, but over the next few days Lydia found herself thinking more and more about the lucrative trade that ran through the streets of Preston, hidden in the back rooms of booksellers and barbers and in the coats and bags of men like Fletcher. Each brown paper package under the arm of a visitor to Kathleen's, each hushed conversation between groups of men in the Bull, made her wonder. One day Henry called at the house, but evidently not for Lydia; he only raised a hand to her briefly before handing Kathleen a pile of new pictures and taking his leave.

When each night's work was over, Lydia stripped off her sour clothes and underthings and sat by the fire in her room, a shawl around her shoulders, scratching out letters and words by the light of the licking flames. Often she would stare into the fire, thinking about Annabel.

With occasional references to some of the papers Lydia borrowed from the parlour, her pen swiftly learned to form the letters of that whole world of words she had known how to speak, but until now had not been able to write: *fuck, cunt*, and a few she couldn't recognize: *orifice, fellatio, coition, phallus.* After reading a few passages with phalluses in them, she came to the conclusion that phalluses were actually cockstands. The pronunciation still eluded her.

Night after night she sat by the fire, her pen trailing across the paper, screwing her face up with the effort of studying extracts of lurid tales about vigorous gallants and amorous harlots with peach-soft thighs bedewed with the spendings of their lovers. Even this smut was written in the hoity-toity language of the quality, and Lydia muttered the strange words to herself over and over again, mastering the language as she scribbled down her own stories.

One night, when she broke off to change the rag in her underclothes, she looked at the dark bloodspots dappling the white cloth—Mary always called them "red flowers"—and thought of her early days in the trade: a freshly deflowered virgin sold as intact. Sitting back down at the fireside and curling into a ball to shield her aching belly, she took up a fresh sheet of paper and began a new story, in which the virginal heroine was broken in and brought to a strange new plateau of ecstasy by a handsome academic with quick, confident fingers.

By the early hours of the morning it was done: three pages of increasingly messy handwriting, with drops of ink spotting the paper where she had paused to study the examples in the papers for guidance as she tried to capture their plummy language. She crawled into bed before she could fall asleep at the hearth.

At lunchtime she went to the Old Bull with Mary, who was meeting Matty. The cherubic lad slid a coin across the table to Mary under the palm of his hand, and she picked it up and tapped it on the wood. It sounded real enough, and the two girls looked at him with raised eyebrows.

"Mm," he said with a nod, pocketing the coin, "I was working on these till quite late last night."

"They're better than your usual," Mary said. "What're you using?"

"Spoons." His voice was quiet, but the proud grin on his face couldn't be contained. "Plain, common pewter spoons. A bloke up from Cardiff told me about it, so I went and bought a few at King's yesterday."

"You should be more careful," Mary scolded. "You'll

give the game away if you're seen buying up all the spoons in town. Her in King's can't mind her own business."

"I need to do something while I'm working on my big plan."

Mary's eyes glittered, and she took Matty's grubby hand. "And what big plan would that be?"

"To earn enough for a house. Then you can leave Kathleen's for good."

Mary cooed and kissed his face, and Lydia tipped her glass, her expression sullen.

Henry did not drop into the Bull for his lunchtime drink that day, and by the time the girls were walking back to the house, irritation buzzed in Lydia's skull like an angry wasp, and the damp ache inside her had set her mood on the very edge of fury. As Mary chattered about her beau, she remained silent and tried to hear only the soothing cadence of her friend's accent.

". . . Ah, maybe he will, though," she finally heard Mary say. "He's a smart lad, maybe he will get us our own place."

"Do you really believe that?" Lydia's tone was almost pleading, and Mary paused.

"I'm not sure. It's a nice thought."

"But do you really want to stay in the trade until Matty finds someone stupid enough to take his money?"

"For sure I do. I'd rather lie on my back than break it."

Lydia nodded. "I'd never choose to sell laces again, but we've hardly got ourselves a trade for life, have we?"

Mary shuddered. "God in Heaven, what a thought! My grandmother lived till she was seventy-three, but I doubt she'd have done it in our line of work." She paused, frowning. "She was a cook," she said finally. "Lost three of her fingers in her time. They had a temperamental old oven, too, and Nan was blinded by fire one day when she tried to light it."

"Don't you want to get out now, while you can still enjoy yourself?" Lydia protested. "There's got to be a way we can earn more than starvation's pay—something we can still do when we're past our best."

Mary frowned, then shattered the seriousness of the moment with a peal of laughter. But her smile didn't reach her eyes.

"Listen to you, girl! A Rescuer got to you?"

"No," Lydia said patiently. Rescuers were do-gooders who cornered girls in the trade and tried to save them, and she felt quite insulted by Mary's insinuation that she would take their prattle seriously. "I'm not talking about shame and sin here. I'm asking if there's a way we can earn ourselves a living that won't dry up when we do." She wrinkled her nose. "And having a choice about which ones we fuck and which we don't would be nice, too."

"Ah, so that's it," Mary crowed.

"What?"

"I told you this whole Mr. Shadwell thing would have an effect soon. You never minded the trade before."

"You talk as if I enjoyed it," Lydia protested.

"Well, well," Mary chuckled. She looked at Lydia mischievously, as though awaiting an explosion of temper, but Lydia just shook her head.

"It's not like you and Matty. At least, I think not. Henry's a nice chap, handsome, too, but—"

"I beg your pardon?" Mary squeaked in protest. Lydia shook her head.

"No, listen. I like Henry well enough, but I don't *know* him, not really. How could I be in love with him?" To her surprise (and horror), she felt her cheeks flush as she spoke. Her guts churned, and she shook her head. "I just feel as if I'm rotting my youth away with fat old men and Kathleen's sponge bucket." She smirked at Mary, and they both giggled. "It's funny today, but I just don't think it will be five years from now."

They turned into the sidestreet where the house stood, and automatically lowered their voices. This was not a conversation for Kathleen's ears.

Mary shrugged. "But who's got time to worry about five years from now? We might not even have that long— why worry yourself sick? It's not as if you were born with many choices." Her words may have been harsh, but her tone was gentle, and Lydia slung an arm around her friend's shoulders and hugged her.

"Thanks for listening."

"Any time," Mary replied. "Just don't tell Herself." She jerked her head towards the parlour window.

"D'you think I'm daft?" Lydia whispered as they made their way into the hall. She was smiling, but in her stomach she felt her resolve harden like cooling steel.

"The Society of Vice, Preston!" Henry exclaimed with pride, two days later. He had collected Lydia from Kathleen's and brought her to his workshop, but he hadn't set up his camera.

Lydia blinked. "What?"

"It's been plaguing me for weeks—this little business of mine really needs a name. The trouble Fletcher and the others have been having with the Society *for the Prevention* of Vice brought out the devil in me. If we're going to have a society to prevent vice, surely we also need one to propagate it." He smirked, sloshing out two glasses of brandy from a flask in his pocket. "All the images I sell from now will bear the Society of Vice's crest, naturally. Much more sophisticated."

"That'll endear you to the other Society," Lydia remarked.

Henry winked. "But they don't know who's behind the pictures, do they?"

Lydia nodded, conceding his point. "So trade really is going well?"

"Wonderfully." Henry beamed. "Due in no small part to your assistance, I'm sure. I haven't had pictures sell like this before."

Distracted for a moment, Lydia felt confused. She knew she wasn't the most stunning girl there was—she was a head taller than both Mary and Daisy, her nose was a little crooked (a result of getting caught up in a fight in the Bull), and her hair—before she twisted strips of cloth into it of a night to try and get some curl in it—was too straight. How could it be that her pictures sold so well?

"I told Kathleen how pleased I was with them," Henry was saying. Then he paused, frowning. "She's an odd woman, isn't she? She looked decidedly suspicious when I told her about the photographs, you know."

Lydia shook her head. "Don't mind her; she's always like this when she thinks one of us is up to something with a man and not being paid for it. She's always going on at me; I think she thinks we're about to elope." She fluttered her eyelashes and laid her head on Henry's shoulder in an elaborate pantomime of devotion.

The remark had been casual enough, but something about Henry's reaction made the back of her neck prickle.

Rather than laughing and returning her caresses, his entire body seemed to tense up against her.

"Henry?" Lydia's voice sounded small and lost. "Henry, what's the matter?"

He stood still and silent for a long moment, before shaking his head.

"Oh, nothing," he said eventually. "I'm sorry, I've just been very busy of late, and it's been occupying my mind. Winter's a bad time for people falling sick. But," he added, "at least it keeps surgeons' hands busy."

This was true. Lydia silently scolded herself yet again— she would not prove Mary right. It didn't matter to her in the least what Henry spent his days doing, she told herself. Then Henry's fingers closed over the bodice of her dress, and she stretched like a stroked cat.

"Not too busy, I hope," she purred.

Afterwards, as they lay tangled up in the sheets on the bed, Lydia realized this was the first time they had both been completely naked together. She delighted in running her fingers across his clean, pale skin. She had soon learned his particular weaknesses—which caresses made him lose all control, which words would incite him to fuck her as if to cling onto life itself. What delighted her most of all was learning which parts of her own body excited him; she could exploit such information mercilessly, nuzzling her breasts against his face, smoothing her thighs against his, offering him her wrists and ankles to nibble and kiss.

They were both exhausted and ravenous, but Lydia had tasted a new power and she could not resist exercising it once more. Straddling his thigh, she rubbed herself against the bristly skin, her head thrown back in release as shock after shock pounded through her. When he snatched her around the waist, every inch of her body hummed with wicked joy.

"Hungry?" he gasped.

Henry had a few things in a basket on his desk, which, he said, he kept handy as he frequently stayed in his workshop until late in the evening. There was a large loaf of bread, a wedge of cheese, some cold chicken and a couple of apples. Lydia devoured everything she was offered, and more than once she noticed Henry watching her as she ate. Her sex flickered in recognition of the dark look of desire in his eyes.

"So," she said, swallowing, "when are we taking the pictures?"

"Hmm?" Henry blinked, as though his thoughts had been elsewhere, but he soon came to his senses. "Oh.

No, I wasn't planning on taking any today—we have plenty to be working with for now."

Lydia wanted to ask why, then, he had brought her here, but she stopped herself. She was quite happy to be lying naked among the sheets with Henry, enjoying her dinner.

"Henry?"

He bit into his apple with a resounding crunch. "Mm?"

"Since your pictures are taking off so well, I thought I might be able to help a little more." Henry was silent, so she pressed on. "I've been working on my writing. I've been looking at the papers you left with Kathleen, and I've started some of my own stories. You could start a paper of your own and put your pictures in them, and I could do stories and the whore guides; you know, tell men where the girls live and how much they cost and what they'll do and all that. It'll be easy for me: I know all the girls in the trade around here."

Henry was watching her intently but Lydia couldn't read his face. Her voice faltered. "And—and you could find an artist, perhaps? To do some drawings? Like the ones you see of dancing girls with their stockings showing, or men's heads just covering their—"

He sighed. "It's an interesting idea, Lydia, but I don't think it'll work."

Her face fell, and Henry started to pat her hair as if she were an excitable horse.

"I have my patients to think of—it's hard enough to

keep a low profile as it is. Only my regular customers know exactly who I am and what I do, and they know that discretion is in everyone's best interests. Publishing such a paper would simply be too risky."

"Well, what if I bring you some of my stories? You could sell them to the papers for me."

"They have their own writers. It wouldn't work." He looked across at her, and she saw the concern seep into his eyes.

"I'm sorry, Lydia. It obviously means more to you than I realized, but you shouldn't worry—your pictures are helping the Society of Vice tremendously."

She dropped her head.

"For what it's worth," he said, "I'd love to hear one of your stories."

A smile spread irresistibly across her face. "But I haven't got them with me."

"Then make one up. A new one."

"Well, whatever pleases you . . ."

For the next hour, Lydia spun a tale as the ideas came to her. She stopped short of making the gent of the piece into a surgeon (indeed, she had burned that story, having been horribly embarrassed by it on second reading), but his physical resemblance to Henry was not at all accidental. This man was an artist, she told Henry: a painter who immortalized his subject's youth and desirability on canvas. She described the slick stroking of the brush through the oils, the proud arch of the girl's neck and the gliding of the paintbrush on the canvas as the artist sought to reproduce it. Henry raised his hand and gently traced the tip of his finger down her neck, and Lydia caught her breath. As she continued with the story, Henry's finger followed the path of the paintbrush down and around the soft white curves of her naked breasts, then circled her nipples as the artist in her story shaded them in a deep rose pink. Together, Henry and the artist in Lydia's story covered the whole of her body—moving over her hips, arms, thighs and the gentle roundness of her belly—before turning their attentions to the soft shadow between her legs, an area which Lydia's fictional artist was particularly diligent about capturing. Again and again Henry's finger followed the path of the paintbrush, until Lydia threw her head back and abandoned herself to the feeling.

When they finally began to dress, Henry reached into the pocket of his coat and withdrew a roll of paper money. Lydia looked blankly at him—she hadn't been paid for shagging Henry in over a fortnight.

"It's all I have on me right now," he explained. He swept her a deep bow, and came up smiling wryly. "If it pleases you to accept it."

Lydia glowed. "Since it's you," she said, tucking the roll of money down between her breasts.

. . .

Mary was sitting alone in the parlour when Lydia went in.

"Ah, you're back." She grinned. "I was beginning to think you'd eloped."

Lydia flopped down on the couch beside her, smiling sarcastically.

"Ooh," Mary said, sniffing Lydia's dress and wrinkling her nose, "I'd do something about that before Kathleen gets back—either have a bath and change your frock, or else make sure you've got some money to show for it."

Lydia had to stop herself holding a lock of her hair to her nose. "Where is Kathleen, anyway?"

"She's looking for . . ." Mary halted awkwardly. "She's out looking for a housemaid. Sorry, Lydia, I didn't mean to remind you about Annie leaving."

"We need someone," Lydia conceded, wondering how her sister was faring. Annie still hadn't written, and Lydia was beginning to doubt that she ever would.

"Kathleen's got a real task on her hands," Mary pointed out, "finding one who don't scream or come over faint if you so much as mention washing our sheets and the sponges."

Lydia chuckled. "She'll find someone. She always gets what she wants. Have you had many blokes while I've been out?"

"Five." Mary held up a hand, fingers spread out. "Five you owe me." This was a system that had been in place for as long as Lydia had been at Kathleen's: if a girl's absence meant more work for another, the favour would be repaid in kind.

Lydia grunted. "Anything unusual?"

"Nah. One of them wanted it backways—that were the last one. I'm definitely taking a break now."

"All right," Lydia said, laughing. "I'm going for a bath."

"Don't be too long," Mary called after her, "I'll be shouting for you if any come."

A couple of minutes later, Mary hollered up the stairs for Lydia. Her bath would have to wait. Determining that the man pacing nervously around the parlour didn't want anything out of the ordinary, she named her price and led him up to her chamber.

"So," he panted after she'd been grinding herself onto him for fifteen minutes, "how did you end up here?"

It was a question she was used to, but she couldn't recall ever having replied honestly. It was just a matter of working out the answer they wanted to hear.

"What d'you mean?" She tried to sound surprised by the question.

"I mean how does a girl end up like you?"

Ah, so he wanted virtue sullied, then. She cast her eyes down and slowed momentarily.

"I was a lady's maid, until my lady's husband decided

he preferred me to his lady. She threw me out when she caught us."

The man's face at that moment was almost comical—a farcical look of sympathy, shot through with his grimace of release.

They were certainly varied, these blokes and their fantasies. Only the other day, she had been a shameless wanton, thrown out by her family for bringing a slur upon their name. She'd loved every minute of it.

As soon as he'd left, she dragged the bath into her room and started lugging buckets of water from the kitchen, before heading back down to heat a large pan on the stove to warm the bath. She could still smell Henry on her skin, but now his scent was overlaid with that of the last man. When the water in the pan came to the boil in a frenzy of bubbles, she wrapped a dishcloth around the handle and heaved it upstairs. But with no Annabel to bring fresh water, the bath cooled quickly, and Lydia got out, wrung her hair over the tub, dressed and made her way downstairs.

Mary looked up as she walked in, but before she could speak, Lydia answered her question with a shake of her head. No, no business worth mentioning. She sat down, picked up the teapot, and gestured to Mary with it.

Mary shook her head. "No. Just finished one."

Lydia shrugged, picked up Mary's leftover cup and sloshed tepid tea into it. As she tipped the cup against her lips, she noticed a ring on Mary's left hand.

"What's that?"

"Matty give it us."

Lydia's eyes widened. "You're never betrothed!"

Mary smiled and shook her head.

"No, we're not. This ring's cheap as they come, it's brass. Matty buys them for threepence a dozen."

"Then why are you wearing it?"

"Because Matty sells them as gold to people passing through the Bull. This way he can show them that he's so proud of what he's selling that he gave one to his girl when he asked her to marry him. Nearly always works." Another pause. "If we were really betrothed, you can bet your life I wouldn't take this ring. Look what it does to my finger!"

She wrenched the ring off and held her hand up to Lydia's face. A mould-coloured green band adorned the base of her finger, and a patch of tiny bumps had begun to irritate the skin.

## 8

When Henry collected Lydia it was the first time she had been out of the house in three days. A heavy snow had fallen, carpeting the streets of Preston in a thick layer that was impossible to walk on in heeled boots. Henry held her arm and she bundled herself into the cab, shivering under her thick wool shawl. As they pulled out of the sidestreet and onto Fishergate, the crowds of shoppers scurried out of the way of the cab-horse's hooves.

Staring dreamily out of the window at the well-lit, inviting shops, Lydia was startled by Henry thrusting a little box under her nose.

"Merry Christmas."

For a moment she was stunned into silence. Christmas

had been a day like any other back when Nell was alive, and although Kathleen always saw to it that her girls got a good dinner that day, in the introduction house they'd never exchanged so much as an orange.

"Well, I'm not holding it in front of your face all day," Henry said wryly. "Open it."

The little box—deep pine green, tied with a white ribbon—felt light in her hand. She pulled the bow loose, letting the ribbon fall into her lap, and opened the box. A pair of pearl earrings nestled on a bed of green velvet. Lydia heard the sharp little hiss of her indrawn breath.

"Go on," Henry said. "I know you want to."

She picked up one of the pearls and clamped it between her teeth. A slight jarring as the hard surface resisted, and a gritty texture against her tongue.

"They're real?"

"They are indeed," Henry replied, his eyes shining. He held out a cupped hand, and she dropped the pearls into his palm. Gathering up her hair, she held it out of the way while he attached the earrings. When she let go of her hair, letting it swish back onto her shoulders, he nuzzled underneath it again, nibbling on the soft, tender skin that fluttered with the pulse on her throat.

"I wish you'd warned me," she said, smiling. "I didn't get anything for you."

Henry lifted her face towards his. Without saying a word, he took hold of her hands in his and laid them over the rigid bulge in the front of his trousers. Peering up from under her lashes, Lydia returned his smile as she began to unbutton him and slid down onto her knees on the floor of the rocking cab.

"D'you still have the energy to take pictures?" she teased as they stepped into Henry's studio.

Henry chuckled, kicking the door closed with one heel.

"Actually, that's not the kind of work I had planned for you today."

"Oh?" Her heart leaped into her throat—had he reconsidered her idea?

"I couldn't stop thinking about our conversation last time we met. You seemed so disappointed." His fingers brushed her arm, and a hot flush ran down the back of her neck.

"I can't possibly start up a paper," Henry said, looking closely at her. "But I do need some assistance with something else—something very important. It must be someone I can trust."

"What?"

He exhaled thoughtfully. "Come with me."

Taking her hand, he led her across the room. The bare floorboards echoed with each step they took. When they stopped in front of the curtain that covered the doorway to the other room, Lydia looked up at Henry in confusion.

"You said I wasn't to go in there!"

"That was then. I need to show my other workshop to you now." Holding the curtain back, he gestured for her to step through.

The room behind the curtain could not have been more different from the one Lydia knew so well. That one was sparsely, tastefully furnished, and the window let in a good light when the sky was bright outside. This space had only a single small window covered by a sheet of heavy paper, and a long, narrow wooden table that took up most of the room. Its top was stained and scarred from years of use and repeated scrubbing. Everywhere there were boxes, and shelves of bottles and jars. There were sketches, diagrams and photographs pinned to the walls, but Lydia couldn't see what they were of. Behind her, Henry reached for an oil lamp that sat on top of a stack of boxes, and gently pushed Lydia further into the room. Her gaze flitted upwards, and she jumped as she caught sight of a pair of eyes glaring down at her from a high shelf.

As the yellow glow of the lamp flooded the room, she realized that the eyes staring at her were dull and unblinking. They belonged to a rather badly preserved stuffed owl, which was shedding its feathers onto the floor.

"I did that a while ago," Henry explained, following her gaze. "Back when I was a student. I found it dead in the road—must've been struck by a carriage—and I thought I could try my hand at taxidermy. Not my best work, as you can see."

Lydia nodded distractedly, but didn't reply. Her eyes swept the room. Jars of cloudy liquid filled the uppermost shelf. Dead mice, unhatched birds of various sizes, a mole, several strange grey masses Lydia couldn't recognize, disembodied human eyes, fingers, hearts. At the end, in a large bottle of thick glass, sat a miscarried infant.

"Where'd you get these?" she breathed.

"Various places. Some I find. The lumpfish roe"—here Henry pointed to one of the greyish lumps—"was given to me by one of my tutors. Some of them I acquire in the course of my work." He reached out and tapped the last bottle. "That was found on the bed of the Ribble by one of the mudlarks. I happened to be passing on my way back from a house call, and he was rather pleased when I offered him two shillings for it. Fascinating, isn't it? Have you ever seen one so well formed?"

Lydia shook her head. "Never seen one this close up before."

"Really?" Henry seemed surprised.

"Kathleen takes care of us."

Lydia turned and walked past the covered window to examine the pictures. A drawing of a human skeleton adorned one wall, next to another of a man with his stomach sliced open and his innards on display. The room's other walls bore yet more sketches: a man's disembodied belly and prick, first disfigured by a bulging hernia, then neatly trussed up; a human head, viewed side-on and sliced straight through to expose bone, brain and muscle; a woman with her arm hanging limply and at a queer angle from her dislocated shoulder, and a surgeon hauling it back into the correct position. Lydia turned away, wincing, and came face-to-face with a photograph of a man with his leg amputated at the hip, with only a sad little row of puckering stitches and the man's dejected expression to show that there had ever been a leg there. On top of a leather-covered chest was a jar half-filled with water, greenish with weeds and housing three long, slug-like creatures.

"Leeches," Henry said, standing at Lydia's shoulder.

Turning back to the table in the middle of the room, Lydia caught sight of another picture, a series of boxes and arrows and words, and in the corner, a photograph of a bearded old man lying on his back. His entire face was consumed by little lumps, and he looked as though he were teeming with maggots. *Smallpox*, the wording below the picture read. Lydia swallowed hard. The back of her throat felt slimy and tasted sharp.

"And this is where my students and I work," Henry said. "You see, a surgeon's life is not one of glamour."

"This is where you treat your patients?"

"Lord, no! But I need somewhere to develop my studies of the body, and to give my anatomy lessons. My students and I meet here once a week."

Lydia nodded slowly. She couldn't stop herself glancing

around the room, taking another look at Henry's collection of pickled artefacts. They were awful, certainly, but there was something compelling about them.

Henry reached over to the end of the table for a bundle of black cloth and unrolled it. Inside were several large knives, the well-used metal glinting dully in the lamplight. Some were small and fine-pointed; others resembled the heavy cleavers Lydia had seen in butcher's shops.

"You cut people up," she said.

"Not people, bodies. I cut the living for their own good, and the dead for the good of the rest of us. How do you think we develop the techniques and cures that heal people and save lives?"

She blinked, staring at the distorted reflection of herself in the wide blade of one of the cleavers. A memory stirred inside Lydia: she was little again, and the workhouse chaplain was delivering one of his sermons before the inmates were allowed to eat their small and unappetizing breakfast. The booming voice echoed down the dining-hall, rattling on about redemption and the Day of Judgment, when the righteous would rise bodily from their graves and up to Heaven.

"So you go to Lancaster, then? For them that get hanged?" She knew the bodies of hanged criminals were given over to the surgeons. She knew that others were used, too, but she held her breath and waited for Henry to tell her that the only bodies hacked up on this table were those whose hopes of a heaven had been snuffed out along with their earthly existence.

"Some of them," Henry replied. "The workhouse provides a fair few, and I'm entitled to the remains of anyone who cannot afford a burial." He looked closely at Lydia. "Don't tell me you're shocked."

"But . . . if you cut up the bodies . . ." She caught sight of Henry. He had raised an ironic eyebrow, and she hesitated. "How is the soul to resurrect?"

Henry opened his mouth, then closed it again, nodding thoughtfully. "You think the body has to be intact for resurrection in the hereafter?"

"Doesn't everyone?"

"People believe all manner of things, Lydia. Tell me—how intact do you think a corpse is after a few years underground?" He held out an arm, pointing out the picture of the one-legged man. "And what about him? Is he damned by his injuries? I cannot afford to pay heed to superstition, and neither can any other man of medicine. And whether they realize it or not, our patients cannot afford to either."

Lydia swallowed. "So," she said, trying to turn the conversation away from the specifics of Henry's anatomy lessons, "what d'you want with me?"

"We have no specimen. I shan't be able to obtain any bodies from the gallows until after the Lent Assizes, and no workhouse inmates or paupers have died this week. Unusual for this time of year."

"You ain't carving me up!" Lydia said it as if she was joking, but her voice shook.

"No, I *ain't*," Henry mimicked. He sighed. "I don't do this often; I'll make that perfectly clear now. Between the gallows and the workhouse, I'm usually well supplied. I haven't had to resort to other means before, but when I was a student, one of my tutors told me how they did things when they were younger. This is why I need your help."

He looked her straight in the eye. His dark gaze was unflinching.

"I want to take you up to the cemetery. Think of it as a kind of reconnaissance mission."

Lydia looked blank, and Henry raked his hand through his hair before continuing.

"You shall pose as a mourner, locate the grave I tell you to find, and note any other details that could prove useful—any gaps in the hedge, any gates or exits other than the main one; you get the idea. Then come back and tell me all about the location—I need to have as clear a picture as possible."

Lydia realized her mouth was open in shock. It was like something out of an old folk tale.

"You want me to plot a grave-robbing for you?"

"If this is going to work, I need someone to go there while it's still light and get a good idea of the area for me."

Lydia took a step back. "You're mad."

Henry shook his head, then leaned back to perch on

the corner of the big table. "Don't think I haven't thought that myself. It's just not something a surgeon has to do nowadays, not since the Anatomy Act granted us the bodies of the paupers and the criminals. But," he continued with a sigh, "here I am without a specimen."

Lydia looked confused. "But you're the teacher, aren't you? Your students can wait till you're ready."

"If only it were that simple. As I told you some time ago, I'm not supposed to teach my skills to laymen, and barbers and apothecaries are as good as laymen in the eyes of the medical profession. If I were found out, the Royal College of Surgeons would strip me of my right to practise. My students have been waiting to complete their studies of the body for a few weeks now, and now one of them is becoming . . ." He smiled halfheartedly. "Impatient."

Lydia nodded. "So you have to find a body, or he blows the whistle on you."

Henry rubbed at an ink stain on one of his fingers. "That's about the size of it, yes."

A shudder ran through Lydia. "I don't know, Henry. This isn't a small favour you're asking—a lot of things I may be, but a body-snatching witch ain't one of them."

"No, I know that. Believe me, Lydia, if I had anyone else to turn to I would not be asking this of you. But either I risk the possibility of being caught stealing a body I'm not entitled to, or I will almost certainly be expelled from the College. Really, there is no choice."

Lydia looked at Henry in silence. For as long as she'd known him, he'd been so cocky about his disregard for professional and social rules, and now he looked so defeated. She wanted to help him, but . . .

"So why can't your bloody student skulk around the cemetery in broad daylight for you then, if he wants his lesson so badly?"

"Because a woman looks less suspicious. My tutor told me he often enlisted the help of a—"

"Whore?"

"A woman such as yourself," Henry finished delicately. "You'll be carrying flowers, of course, just as if you were visiting a grave." He nodded towards a bunch of white lilies in a flask of water on the shelf.

"A whore in a red dress with a bunch of flowers? Oh yes, I'm sure I'll pass for a heartbroken sweetheart just perfectly."

He reached over into a shadowy corner of the room and tossed Lydia a bundle of black. She held the mourning dress by the shoulders and shook it out. A cheap black lace veil was tucked into one of the sleeves, stiff and scratchy.

"I've been asked to wear some unusual things before now, Henry Shadwell, but this takes the prize."

He chuckled. "So you'll do it?"

She couldn't help but notice that it wasn't really a question. "I can't believe I'm doing this—all this fuss about the Ripper and I start knocking about with a southerner with a collection of dead things in jars! Which poor sod am I helping you uproot? God, Henry . . ."

"Don't worry about who it is," he soothed, slipping his skilled fingers into the hollows beneath her shoulders and working them into the tense muscle.

Despite herself, Lydia felt her neck and back loosen, and her shoulders dropped a little. Sensing her weakening, Henry slipped her dress from her shoulders and worked the bodice down around her waist so he could slip his hands into the top of her corset. His teeth closed gently on one of her new pearl earrings, before trailing around to the scruff of her neck, where he sucked urgently on the flesh below her hairline.

"Is this why you got me the earrings?" Lydia murmured. Her gaze fell once more on the rows of jars and the grisly treasures within; her voice was low and reluctant. Henry shook his head, reaching down to unbutton her dress and let it fall into a heap at her feet.

"On my honour, no."

"I'm not inclined to trust your honour," she said, leaning back against him.

The mourning dress fitted Lydia fairly well, although it was a little tight across her bosom. She thought she looked ridiculous in it.

"You look perfectly fine," Henry assured her. "You're

simply not used to wearing something with such a high collar. You will certainly look suspicious if you weep over a grave with your breasts on display."

"Oh, I have to weep now, do I?"

"Just so long as you look as if you're mourning."

Lydia pressed her hand to her forehead and sighed melodramatically. "*Oh, my love! My love! Taken from us far too soon!* There, that do?"

Henry laughed. "Actually, the one you're looking for would be more likely to be your grandfather, and I doubt the locals who knew of him would have agreed that he was taken from us far too soon. You see, he—"

Lydia cringed. "Don't tell me about him! I can do this if I must, but the less you tell me about the poor devil whose body you're stealing, the better."

"Really, you shouldn't be concerned. I'll explain everything tomorrow. But now," he said, reaching for his waistcoat and digging his watch from the pocket, "I must dash; I have an appointment. D'you want a ride into town?"

The cab dropped them on Winckley Square and Henry nodded a quick farewell to Lydia before hurrying across the road towards the large houses just off the square. Lydia, stung, reminded herself that he had to present a certain image to his wealthier patients—he had certainly dressed well in preparation for this appointment. She looked over at the imposing faces of the big houses and gritted her teeth. An uneven weight in one of her pockets—the roll of money Henry had given her the other day—knocked against her thigh as the winter winds gusted past.

Shivering, she stepped through the gate of the gardens and started to cut across. Whenever there was a break in the foliage, a blast of icy air attacked Lydia, leaving her ears aching and her cheeks feeling as though they had been slapped. A plump, richly dressed lady was standing with a maid in the shelter of an oak tree, watching a small, fluffy white dog digging in a bare flowerbed. Lydia watched the creature's industrious efforts, its grubby paws flying back and forth, shuddering as she remembered Henry's plans for tomorrow. He had told her to get plenty of sleep—he would need her with him all day, and he would pay Kathleen for the trouble.

Voices ahead made her look up, and her heavy heart leaped as she recognized her sister. Annie had grown taller—thinner, too, but sometimes girls her age went through a straggly phase. Her neatly tied hair was resisting the wind better than Lydia's tousled mess, and she walked with her head down, looking at her feet. A tall, thin man in fine clothes walked beside her, and Lydia deduced that this must be Mr. Hollingworth. The twin girls were walking with them, and Annie kept an almost theatrically diligent watch over them, barely turning to face Mr. Hollingworth when he spoke to her.

His hands moved periodically as he spoke, and every time he raised them, Annie moved, shying away ever so slightly. One of the girls kept skipping off the path and onto the grass to inspect a fallen leaf or a snail shell, but the other seemed dull and sullen, walking with her chin on her chest and frequently muffling a cough with her shawl. Lydia wished that the weather were milder so she could read more in her sister's face: her eyes were downcast and her skin flushed, but this wind would have that effect on anyone.

As Annie and the Hollingworths turned, an evergreen bush blocked Lydia's view. She could just see the top of Mr. Hollingworth's head as he addressed Annabel, and then turned to call to the girls. Lydia froze as his gaze fell across her. She swore under her breath and continued walking. Mr. Hollingworth's piercing blue gaze passed over her once more, before he appeared to lose interest and turn away. Then Annie turned and looked and Lydia beamed, raising her hand.

Her sister paled. Without so much as a nod, she turned her eyes back to her feet until she was out of sight.

# 9

Lydia did not return to the introduction house straight away. Instead, as she made her way back along Fishergate, she turned down Glovers Court. It was a narrower road, little more than a sidestreet really, and the tall buildings on either side closed it in, making it even darker in the dying light of the winter afternoon. Lydia picked her way down the sloping cobbled road, placing her feet carefully so that she wouldn't fall over in her heeled boots and twist an ankle. Henry might not think her idea was worth a try, but she'd be damned if she'd let that stop her.

Stanley Stoker's printing shop wasn't the sort of place you'd find without local knowledge, but Lydia, remembering the earlier conversation with John Fletcher, walked slowly down Glovers Court, her eyes darting from one side of the road to the other in search of Fletcher's bookshop. Finally, she spotted a small leaded window, behind which sat a small display of bound books: Bibles, novels and encyclopedias. Lydia looked up to the curtainless window above, but she could see no sign of a business operating there. Looking back up the street, she spied a costermonger standing outside the Wellington Inn a few doors away, gulping down a pint while guarding his barrow.

"Is the printworks above here?" she asked, jerking her head towards the shop window. The costermonger nodded.

"There's a flight of stairs just inside the shop door. He should be there at this hour."

Lydia thanked him and ducked through the door of Fletcher's shop.

The printer had heard her coming up the stairs, and met her at the door of his shop. Ink stained every surface, and crates of paper and playbills and pamphlets were scattered across the floorboards. Stanley Stoker's gaze swept over Lydia. He wasn't a young man—older than Kathleen, certainly—but he wasn't decrepit either, although he stooped when he stood, probably from years of bending over the presses. There were a couple of younger men in the shop, too, one winding the rollers of an object that resembled a mangle, the other picking tiny letters from a wooden box and setting them into an iron frame.

"I hear you print some of the local gents' papers," she said, without introducing herself.

The man hesitated only momentarily. "Aye." It was true what Kathleen had told Lydia: Stan the Frenchman was about as French as an Eccles cake. "Only on a letterpress, mind: I'm a jobbing printer really, so I don't have all the large equipment they use for books and newspapers these days." He nodded in the direction of the lad working the mangle-like contraption. A steady stream of headed notepaper emerged from between its wheels, and the young man carefully picked each sheet up in turn and laid it out on a nearby workbench for the ink to dry. "That's my bread and butter, there: the jobbing platen. Mostly I print up posters and bills and tickets and the like, and letterheads like that one there of course. The letterpress is old-fashioned for papers, really, but it'll do you for a few sheets."

Lydia watched as the man picking letters paused to consult the handwritten page in front of him, before continuing with his painstaking composition. The thought of laying out just one of her stories letter by letter made her head ache, but the printer's assistant seemed used to it. She nodded decisively.

"I'm starting one. A paper, I mean. What'll you want to print it for me?"

Stanley Stoker puffed thoughtfully and chewed a

blue-black fingernail. "Depends. How long d'you plan on it being? How many pictures? With the letterpress you've got to stick to lithographs, mostly, although we do have quite a few different stock plates you can choose from. And then there's the fonts."

Lydia swallowed hard, squirming inwardly. She wondered if everyone else who sought out Stoker's business understood these exotic terms, or if they just pretended to.

"Just tell me how much it'll cost to print up something like"—she improvised, snatching up a copy of *Onan* from a shelf nearby—"like that, say. Like that."

Stoker put down the pile of paper. "Follow me."

In the Wellington, they sat down with a couple of mugs of ale and Stan spread sheets of paper out over the sticky tabletop. Most of the papers contained two or three stories per issue, he explained (plus any other writing such as guides to the local girls or skits on the Society), but it was best not to have more than one or two pictures, if you wanted to keep your printing costs down.

"I've a box full of plates with the sort of pictures you might be wanting," he said, lowering his voice. At once, Lydia drew back, expecting him to reach for her, but the printer's gaze was following a couple of men passing by their table, and Lydia realized that his priority was secrecy. Once the men had moved away, Stan continued.

"You should be able to sell 'em for twelve shillings apiece; that's what most of the papers I print go for. You won't be getting so many fonts on the letterpress as you would on the platen, neither, but I can do your title in something nice." He laid a sheet in front of her, with five lines of different fancy type. "What is your title, by the way?"

Lydia took a gulp of ale and licked her lips. She hadn't thought to come up with a title until the previous night. She had never really thought of how these things had been done for the other gents' papers: who had come up with *Onan* or *The English Vice*, or requested that a little lithograph of a ladybird be set atop the header of *The Gentlemen's Review*. But last night, as she had been turning the matter over and over in her mind, her thoughts had turned to Henry's quick fingers moving against her soft, slick flesh, and when she remembered the expression Mary used for the curse, Lydia's mind was made up. She set down her mug with affected casualness.

*"The White Flowers Reader."*

Stan looked blank, and Lydia realized that she was tapping the tabletop with a fingernail. Licking her dry lips, she continued. "And I want a line under that: *The exploits of a Lancashire rose*. Or something like that." She stared at the page of fonts in front of her, not looking up at Stan. One of them looked strong and steady, as if the sturdy capitals had been hewn from solid oak, and Lydia laid a finger down on it.

"In that one. I like that one."

Finally they managed to reach an agreement, and Lydia stuck her hand across the table to meet Stan's.

"Done."

When she arrived back at the house, Kathleen was waiting for her, a note clutched in one hand. Since Henry was to need her for the whole of the next day, the abbess had decided that Lydia should handle most of the trade for the rest of the afternoon.

"If there's any whipping boys or ones that prefer blonde girls I'll get Mary, but otherwise you can deal with them," she said. She eyed the note in her hand with a look of unease. "I can't really complain about all the time you spend with this Mr. Shadwell, not if he's paying up fairly." Her eyes narrowed. "He is paying for everything, isn't he?"

Lydia cleared her throat as quietly as she could. At times like these she was grateful that very little made her blush any more. Still, the abbess's eye was sharp; she seemed to know her girls inside out. Lydia had a feeling Kathleen had guessed Mary's real reason for visiting the Bull so often, and surely it was only a matter of time before her own dealings with Henry were exposed.

"Of course," she spluttered.

Kathleen looked steadily at her. "I know a fancy when

I see it, and I know damn well that you've got a bit of a thing for him. Just you remember, you're not his sweetheart."

"I told you, we ain't been doing anything."

"I hope to God that ain't true, either," Kathleen said as Lydia clomped up the stairs. "You won't make a living that way."

She had been hoping for a quiet afternoon so that she could practise her writing, but it was not to be. Far from slaking their lust, the cold weather had driven those men who would normally have made do with a street-walker into the warmth of the introduction houses. Lydia listened to the familiar sound of an argument drifting up the stairs as Kathleen refused to haggle. No sooner had one man pulled out of her body than another was tapping at her door. Her muscles ached from clenching around them in an attempt to feign her own excitement and speed along theirs.

When the eleventh had made a rather awkward exit, she lay back on the bed in her corset and petticoats, her arms flung wide and her hips aching. Another knock at the door elicited an exhausted groan before she could stop herself.

"All right, only me." Mary's grinning face peered

around the door, and she laughed at the sight of Lydia spread out on the rumpled bed.

"Jesus, no wonder you're tired—how many was that?"

"Eleven," Lydia groaned.

"God! I lost count after seven." Mary grinned. "So what are you and Mr. Shadwell getting up to tomorrow, then?"

Lydia grimaced. "Oh, I don't want to talk about it; I don't even want to *think* about it. God knows what sort of trouble he's going to get us into."

"Can't be worse than Matty—he's got me buying spoons for him how, so her in King's doesn't suspect!"

Lydia frowned. "You silly cow, are you trying to go down for coining, too?"

"No, but what choice do I have? He's going to need the spoons whoever buys them, and this way he's less likely to get caught, which means I'm less likely to get caught."

Lydia fell silent. She could hardly object to Mary helping her beau forge coins when the night before she had promised to help hers steal a body from its grave.

"Oh, I should get some sleep, I suppose," she said. "But not before I've had a bath." She plucked at the petticoats clinging to her thighs, an expression of distaste on her face.

"I'll fetch it for you if you want," Mary said amiably, reaching across to tuck Lydia's breasts back into the top of her corset, "but you'll have to help us with the water."

The noise of a burglary in the street outside woke her early, and after shuffling out onto the landing to squint at the clock, she deduced that there was little point in going back to bed. Reaching for the candle at the side of her bed, she fumbled around in her top drawer for the matches and lit the wick. A lonely glow emanated from the top of the candle, struggling in the early morning cold.

The bill from Stan the Frenchman was still lying on her pillow where she'd been admiring it as she fell asleep: a little creased now, but comforting all the same. A fading memory of the dreams she'd had were still there in her mind's eye: for some reason they'd been of Nell's calloused hands dealing cards onto an upturned barrel, back when Lydia was little and her mother had got it into her head to teach her how to spread the broads. Lydia pushed the thought of Nell from her mind and rubbed the sleep from her eyes, looking again at the bill in front of her.

*Stoker & Sons Printing Office. Billheads, posters, tickets, stationery etc. Quality printing delivered in a timely manner & at a moderate cost.* There was a royal crest on there, too, but Lydia doubted that Her Majesty would trouble to send word up to the likes of Stan the Frenchman every time she needed more headed paper. But underneath that, there it was: the order for two hundred copies of *The White Flowers Reader*. Lydia had paid half the sum she owed already, and had promised to drop her pages in at the printworks in the next few days. She would pay the rest of her account when her papers were ready.

Christ, it was cold. The cheap mourning clothes Henry had given her were sitting on top of her dresses in her clothes chest, and she wriggled into them, cursing the shoddy, itchy fabric. She would leave the veil off until they got to the graveyard—she didn't want to be more conspicuous than she already was. As an afterthought, she dug a voluminous green cape out of her chest, put it on over the mourning weeds and checked her reflection from all angles in the mirror. Satisfied that her dress was sufficiently concealed, she sat down on the bed to await Henry's arrival.

She didn't wait long. Kathleen shouted up to her just after Lydia heard a knock at the front door, and was waiting with Henry in the parlour when she came downstairs.

"I thought you'd overslept—not having any breakfast?" Kathleen asked.

Suppressing a wave of nausea, Lydia shook her head. She noticed Henry studying her green cape, and she casually flicked a corner of it back so he could see the black underneath.

"Well, we'd best be off, Mrs. Tanner," he said. "Shall we settle up tomorrow, when we know how long I need to pay you for?"

Kathleen nodded, one eyebrow raised ever so slightly.

"Right," Henry said once they were safely settled in the back of the cab. "We'll go right now—it's going dark so early at the moment."

"Hmm," Lydia grunted.

"The one you're looking for," Henry said, plucking the black lace veil from her hand and pinning it to her hair, "is the recently deceased John Cutts. Is the name familiar to you?"

Lydia shook her head.

"Well, John Cutts lived a long life, ate well and could afford a decent burial—"

"What've I said about telling me about him?" she cried.

"Be quiet a minute and listen. John Cutts, as I was trying to tell you, made his living as a grave-robber while the demand was there, as did his father before him. I saw his obituary in the paper—placed by his family, of course, and with no mention of his activities. Apparently he owned a small business selling gardening tools in his later years." Henry chuckled. "You can't fault his humour, at least. So you'll be doing nothing the man himself didn't do while he was alive, and for a pretty penny too. I saw his obituary in the paper and recognized the name: old George, one of my students, knew of him when he was a lad, and his father too. The police had their suspicions, but the Cutts family were careful and they could never prove anything. Hopefully if I *am* caught, they will go easier on me."

Lydia looked levelly at Henry, but he would not meet her eye. She decided not to express her doubts—better to let him believe whatever he needed to. Eventually, he looked up at her.

"Are you sure you're willing to do this?"

Lydia smiled ruefully. "No, but let's do it anyway."

Henry's face was still, but his eyes held Lydia's. "Perhaps I did the wrong thing, asking you to help me," he said gently. "I should have known that it would be far more, well, personal for someone with . . . with your background."

Lydia shrugged. "It's nothing I haven't been thinking about ever since my ma died."

"Your mother was given to the surgeons?"

"That's what I'm s'posing. She made us leave before she died, so we wouldn't go into the workhouse. I've no idea how long it took them to find her." When Lydia blinked, a picture of Nell's face, coated in moss and mould, surfaced in her mind, and she swallowed down her urge to vomit.

Henry laid a tentative hand over hers. "I'm sorry,

Lydia. I just needed someone I could trust, and who wouldn't raise suspicion, and would be able to read the tombstones . . . I didn't think."

Lydia shook her head. "I'm here, ain't I?"

"We've arrived," he whispered eventually. Lydia nodded vigorously.

"I'll be fine." She laughed, and her lip trembled.

"Take your time," Henry said, lowering his voice to a whisper. "Find the grave, and look out for any unusual markers—angels and the like. Leave the flowers on the grave—they'll be a useful marker—and don't forget the quickest and most discreet ways in and out. Remember, we'll be doing this in the dark."

To Lydia's surprise, he took her face in his hands and kissed her firmly on the mouth.

"I trust you, Lydia. Good luck."

With the bunch of lilies clutched tightly in her trembling fingers, Lydia made her way through the black gate into the cemetery. She wondered how Henry was planning on getting in once the gate had been locked up for the night—it was too tall to vault or even climb, especially with night-frost coating the railings. Still, the railings around the sides of the cemetery were considerably lower, although they did have pointed tips that would require careful negotiation in the dark.

To her right, there was a space in the hedging, just around the gates. It wasn't much, but if anyone were to walk past at the wrong time, they'd be able to see in. The trees that grew inside the fence were only saplings, so no cover there.

*Never mind all the obvious stuff around the gates*, she chided herself, *he wants to know about the grave*. Picking her way over a frozen puddle on the path in front of her, she strode on in what she hoped was a purposeful manner, all the while flicking her eyes left to right in search of new headstones.

On she walked, past graves laid out in neat rows like terraced houses, almost identical markers of stone or marble, looking, she thought, like doorways into the underworld. Occasionally she saw the tall pillar of a monument, or a great slab the size of a marriage bed lying flat on the ground—a family tomb. The flowers at some of the gravesides looked fresh, and as Lydia thought of the grieving relatives who would have left them, a shudder slithered through her body. She tightened her grip on the lilies in her hand and walked on.

Then she saw it: a smooth stone in black marble with John Cutts's name newly carved, standing out crisp and white. There was already a single white lily lying on the freshly turned soil, and Lydia looked over her shoulder in case any of his relatives were still around. But the only eyes she met were the blank white orbs of a marble angel—rather showy, Lydia thought, as she stared back at it. She turned away and walked up to Cutts's graveside, her eyes flitting left to right as she mentally noted the names of the people buried on either side.

The wind was biting through the cheap black frock Henry had given her, and in her haste to get back to the warmth of the cab, Lydia stumbled. As she did so, she came face to face with a man standing up to his shoulders in an open hole. His head poked above the ground like a worn, weathered old monument, and Lydia clapped a hand over her mouth before she could shriek in surprise.

"I beg your pardon, miss," the gravedigger said hurriedly. "I didn't mean to startle you."

Lydia drew a deep breath to compose herself. "I was surprised, that's all." She was amazed to see now that he had removed his cap in her presence: a gesture of respect she had never experienced before. Then again, she'd never been dressed like a respectable and recently bereaved young woman before.

. . .

Henry was waiting with a pencil and paper when she got back into the cab.

"So, what did you find?"

Lydia relayed everything she could remember. It sounded so disjointed and patchy when she tried to explain it, but Henry seemed satisfied as he sketched a rough map of the cemetery and scrawled landmarks around it.

"There's a big vault nearby," she explained. "Reynolds, I think it was. Then there's a Sedgewick and a Black to Cutts's left, and . . ." She screwed up her face as she tried to remember the others. "Fisher, that were it! A Fisher and a Metcalf to the right. There's an angel as well, and there's not many of them in the area, so that should help."

When she fell silent, Henry folded the paper several times into a tight little square and pushed it into a buttoned pocket in his waistcoat.

"That's wonderful. You're quite extraordinary, you know."

Lydia exhaled heavily. "So they say."

"I mean it," Henry protested. "Why do you do this every time I try to be nice to you?"

Lydia's chin was on her chest. "Not used to people saying nice things to me and meaning it, I suppose," she muttered. "They always want something from me."

Henry didn't reply straight away, but regarded Lydia with an expression of cool interest that made her feel like one of his specimens floating in a bottle.

. . .

Back at the boarding-house, Henry jiggled his key in the creaking lock of his workshop while Lydia tore the scratchy veil from her hair. Inside, the camera was standing ready in the middle of the room, and all the little ladylike props were scattered artfully about the place. Lydia draped her green cape over a box of photographs. Her fingers moved automatically towards the buttons of her dress.

"Are we doing more pictures, then?"

Henry shook his head. "No. At least, not any more. I had planned to take some, but . . ."

"But what?"

Henry approached her in silence. She could smell the rich scent of him as he moved closer to her and laid an arm about her waist. His hand rested on her back, and her skin prickled under the itchy mourning frock. He nuzzled his face against hers until she followed his lips with her own, seeking out the kiss that always—barely—evaded her. She ran her tongue along the roof of her mouth in anticipation.

"Lie down and lift your skirts," Henry whispered huskily. Lydia shook her head.

"Get me out of this bloody dress—I can't stand it another minute."

Henry unbuttoned the dress with one nimble hand. Lydia sighed in relief as the prickly black fabric fell from her shoulders, and she wriggled her hips to shake it down off her waist. Underneath, her arms were pink from scratching, and she clawed at her skin.

Henry pushed her back onto the bed, and she stretched out and let her head fall to one side. The curtain that covered the doorway to his dissection room had been pulled back, and she could just about make out the silhouette of the ragged owl. Henry pushed her petticoats up around her waist and ran his fingertips over her drawers, making her squirm in anticipation.

He pulled his hands away, and made no move to free himself from his trousers. Looking down into her eyes, he asked a question as if he had only just thought of it.

"You lost your virginity young?"

Catching her breath, Lydia stared back at him. "'Course I did—well, not as young as some, but still."

"And you have taken men in your hand? In your mouth?"

"You know I have."

"And they've taken you other ways?"

She tried not to groan. She'd eventually lost her conviction that she would be torn asunder whenever a catch insisted on having it through the back door, but she'd been extremely relieved when Henry had shown no interest in it. Some of her distaste must have shown on her face, though, because Henry laughed.

"No, no, that's not what I'm going to do. I'm a cunt man, I assure you."

Before she could react, Henry dropped his face between her legs, as if to suck her. She gasped in shock as he pushed against her aching skin, nuzzling and lapping at the fabric until it clung to her body, teasing and tormenting her. He moved his face against her, and the strong, straight line of his nose caught her in the strange, throbbing place his fingers had. Lydia cried out, reaching her arms up above her head to grip the bedframe.

Henry caught her around the waist as she writhed, and pulled her drawers down. Whisking them from her ankles, he tucked them into the pocket of his waistcoat and caught hold of her thighs, pulling them further apart. He looked down at her, and Lydia caught her breath.

For a moment, when his mouth touched her bare flesh, she believed she had gone quite mad. Her whole body seemed to melt with a fierce pleasure unlike any she had ever known, and she felt sure she was floating inches above the rumpled sheets. Only the very core of her body felt real, and tiny lightning bolts seemed to strike her with each touch of his tongue. She gripped the bedposts until her fingers went white. She had no words to describe what she felt. The roughness of Henry's beard was indescribable against her softest parts, and his tongue seemed able to melt into her and thrust against her at the same time. Whenever he moved his head, the part of her sex he had just been kissing stung in protest.

When he rested his forehead on her belly, Lydia heard herself sigh. Henry slipped a finger into her, and she squeezed against it gratefully as he swirled the tip inside. Then he drew himself up and lay along the length of her body, and kissed her mouth. She tasted her musk on his tongue; a pleasurably peculiar taste. She had tasted herself on Henry's organ before, but this was just her; the familiar scent of her body thickened on the back of her tongue. Lydia let her head fall back on the bed and gave herself up to the strange, floating sensation.

The warmth of Henry's palm on the curve of her belly stirred her, although she had no idea how much later.

"I take it you've never had that done to you before?"

She shook her head. She'd had men prodding and invading her down there, staring at her as if she were an animal in a zoo, caged for their amusement, but never before had she come close to feeling this way. Her skin shimmered with a light dew, and every time she moved, a memory of her recent pleasure came back to her.

"No," she said finally.

# 10

She dozed lightly until darkness fell. Occasionally she stirred, remembering where she was, and looked around for Henry. Once she heard the clanking of metal and glass from his dissection room, but, too sleepy to move, she huddled herself around a pillow and drifted off again.

Late in the afternoon, Lydia finally sat up. A cold draught was blowing through the crack under the door, and outside she could hear the people scurrying around the docks, cursing each other and calling out Christmas greetings.

Henry emerged from the other room, polishing a metal instrument on a stained rag.

"Good morning," he said, grinning.

Lydia rubbed her face, pushing tangles of hair from her eyes, and looked out of the window. An inky blue winter dusk coloured the sky, and she grunted in acknowledgement of Henry's jest.

"What time is it? When are the others coming?"

"Not for hours yet."

"Are you sure you want me with you?"

"Yes. I want you to understand exactly what I'm doing—if all you have in your head is half-truths, you'll torture yourself with them. You're a tough girl, I know you'll cope."

As they dressed for the arrival of Henry's students, Lydia realized that she would have to wear the hated mourning weeds again.

"I should've brought another dress with me—God knows how long I'll be sat in the graveyard in this sodding thing," she grumbled.

"You'll be much less likely to be seen in black than in red." He tugged Lydia's hair playfully. "Come along, dear—do medicine a favour."

The four students arrived as Henry's watch struck half past twelve. Lydia realized she had been expecting more. She'd been introduced to them briefly—two apothecaries, Gerard and Kendall, and two barber-surgeons, a father-and-son duo called George and Robert. The barbers, Lydia decided, seemed like decent enough blokes, but there was something sly about Kendall the apothecary, and she suspected it was he who had threatened Henry with exposure. As soon as he had walked in, his pale blue eyes had been on her like a ferret on a rat, and Lydia gulped down the nasty taste that suddenly flooded her mouth.

It was clear that none of the men knew how to react to Lydia's presence. The other apothecary, Gerard, Lydia would have known anywhere as Mary's whipping boy from the day she met Henry. The young man would not meet her eye, but at the sight of her, he and Kendall had exchanged meaningful looks, and Robert had stared at his shuffling feet. George, however, seemed determined not to look at Kendall at all, and instead busied himself straightening the specimen jars on Henry's shelves.

"So, Shadwell," Kendall began, as they emerged from the workshop with bundles of tools and filthy blankets. "Very good of you to bring a friend along to keep us company."

Henry closed his eyes briefly. "Yes, Lydia helped me to plot out the area."

"Amazing what you can get some girls to do for money, isn't it?" His eyes gleamed at Lydia, ratlike, from under a dishevelled lock of colourless hair. "Anything for a couple of shillings, eh?" He ran the tip of his tongue along his thin lips.

"Not quite anything," she said, meeting his narrow

eyes. With a sweet smile, she stalked off to find her green cape.

"If you want to find yourself a whore, Kendall, please do it in your own time," she heard Henry say. "Besides, I doubt your wage could stretch to Lydia."

Biting her lips to stop herself laughing, Lydia swept through the door that Henry held open for her.

It was bitterly cold that night. As the open cart rattled through the crooked little streets of workmen's houses, Lydia could hardly make out the shape of her own hand in front of her face, but as they moved further into town, through the richer districts, some light shone through the curtains. She pulled her cape closer and shivered. Beside her, Henry laid a hand on her thigh as she tried to still her chattering teeth. She leaned against him to share the warmth of his body.

The roads were quiet, save for the occasional drunk or gaggle of streetwalkers. As they crossed the bridge beside the railway station, Lydia spied the tall hat of a peeler bobbing slowly towards them and nudged Henry. He muttered under his breath to Robert, who was driving the cart, and they turned casually down an uneven sidestreet and rattled along until they could rejoin the main road.

Leaving the town behind them, they approached the

shadow of the cemetery. Robert pulled the horse to a halt outside the main gate and they piled down off the back of the cart. Lydia hesitated as Henry held out a hand to help her down. The grubby bundle of tools was tucked under his other arm. George, who was taking his son's place at the reins, looked back at them, with sympathy in his eyes.

"I'll look after Lydia as well if you like, Henry," he said gently. "Whatever you think best."

Henry's voice was firm yet gentle. "Come on, Lydia. We talked about this, didn't we? Whatever you're imagining will be far worse than what is about to happen, I'm almost certain of that."

Lydia sighed. Taking Henry's hand she jumped down, flexing her knees as she landed on the cobbles. George clicked his tongue and the horse clopped slowly around the corner, melting into the shadows.

"Right," Henry whispered. "Let's get out of the road."

The imposing steel gate was secured with a thick chain and lock: the noise they would make if they tried to climb over would wake anyone sleeping nearby. *Well, almost anyone*, Lydia thought, eyeing the black outline of a tombstone through the fence. The iron railings marking the southern boundary were lower, however, and Henry rubbed the palm of one of his gloved hands over a couple of them, sweeping away the frost. The rat-faced apothecary took hold of the fence and raised his boot, but Henry stopped him and pushed Lydia towards the fence.

"Ladies first," he said, glaring at Kendall's raised eyebrow. He clasped his hands together, like grooms did when helping women of quality mount their horses.

"Go on, quickly, before someone comes."

She set her boot into his hands, and clambered carefully over the railings with Henry's help, taking care not to catch herself or her dress on their pointed tips. She shuddered as a gust of wind rushed towards her from between the headstones. Wrapping her velvet cape tighter around herself, she stamped her feet as quietly as she could on the frozen ground.

Henry tossed the bundle of tools over to Lydia and scrambled over the iron railings, followed by the three remaining students.

After walking for ten minutes, Henry looked up from the crude map and turned to Lydia.

"It's around here, isn't it?" he whispered, taking the tools from her. "Didn't you say it was two or three along from that vault?"

Glancing over at the bed of stone covering the Reynolds family tomb, Lydia nodded and, with the others in pursuit, walked away from the fence and the wind-tossed hedges and towards the huge grey slab. She stepped up onto the top of the vault and walked over it. The sound of her boots on the slab was heavy and solid, and she found it hard to believe that barely a few feet below her was a tiny, airless room stacked with coffins containing generations of mouldering relatives. Lydia, born in an overcrowded sickhouse, raised in a single room and frequently sharing her bed with strangers, couldn't imagine why anyone would want company while the worms picked their bones clean.

She raised a hand to Henry and silently indicated John Cutts's grave. Further into the cemetery, a fox slithered in between two old markers, one broken and leaning against the other. The lone angel that had startled Lydia with its dead gaze cast a cold look down upon the party assembling at the graveside. Henry tossed the rolled-up blanket down, the metallic chink of the tools inside blown away on the wind.

"Do you have the matches?" he asked one of the men. Crouching down in the shadow of the gravestone, he fumbled with an oil lamp, lighting it and carefully draping it with a hood of black felt. A neat hole in the fabric shone a beam of light straight onto the ground atop the grave. The men set about unrolling another bundle, and Lydia watched as a pick, a wooden spade, a coil of thick rope and two hammers and chisels were tossed onto the hard ground, and the empty blanket spread out at the graveside.

"Take shelter by the trees," Henry said to Lydia, nodding towards a cluster of baby oaks.

When she reached the cluster of trees, she tested the ground with her fingertips before deciding that it was too cold and wet to sit down. Leaning back against one of the sturdier saplings, she huddled into her cape and strained her eyes in the darkness. The felt hood Henry had fitted onto the lamp had done its job—it took Lydia a few moments to spot Henry and his students a few yards away. Robert was driving the edge of the spade lightly into the topsoil, breaking and loosening it. Surely they wouldn't be seen from the road, even if someone were to pass at this late hour?

Lydia, shivering in the cold and trying in vain to stop her teeth chattering, glared at the cold, indifferent features of the angel that stood sentinel over the light of the lantern. The orange glow was faint, but if she watched closely enough, she could see the soil piling up on the sheet beside them.

The wind dispersed nearly all sound from the men working at the grave. Squinting, Lydia could make out lumps of clay on top of the pile of frozen topsoil. They must be getting close. Finally, Henry—still silent—reached across for the rope, and Lydia found herself tiptoeing away from the cover of the trees and a little closer to the men. Safely hidden behind the tall column of a family monument, she watched as Henry and Robert lowered themselves into the grave. Lydia wrapped her arms around the cold stone pillar and watched as the men standing at the grave's edge handed down the hammers and chisels.

The rhythmic clanking of the coffin lid being driven loose made her cringe and cling more tightly to the pillar. Then she sighed in relief at the crack of the lid coming loose, and the silence descended again. Henry climbed out and stood with his back to Lydia. With her view blocked, she couldn't see what happened next, until Henry moved aside to fetch the second filthy roll of blanket.

In the shielded light of the lantern, she could see the limp form of John Cutts being hoisted from his grave, a rope tied under his arms and around his chest. Henry wrapped his end of the rope around the headstone and pulled until his students could roll the body out onto the grass. Looking over his shoulder, Henry saw Lydia and beckoned, pulling a small flask from his pocket and offering it to her. Glaring at Lydia, Kendall picked up the spade and started shovelling soil back into the hole, on top of the shattered coffin. She sniffed the liquor before taking a belt, and wrinkled her nose at the sight of the flaccid body being flopped onto the blanket and rolled up like a rug. She had expected a smell, but in the frosty air of the open graveyard, any odour the body might have had was blown away, leaving only the ominous presence of the rolled-up blanket to betray what had happened.

The body lay rolled in the blanket in the back of the cart. When Henry passed his flask around, Kendall half-drained it, then busied himself telling Lydia jokes she'd already heard about places called Maidenhead, Staines and Virginia Water.

"I thought they were stiff," Lydia murmured to Henry.

"Only for a while," Henry replied. "It soon passes, and then they soften again."

Kendall grinned idiotically. He did not appear to be at all fearful of the risk his demands had brought to them all.

"I think you've had enough of this," Henry remarked, plucking the flask from Kendall's hand. He shook it, sighed, and tossed what was left to George.

Kendall tapped Lydia on the shoulder. "What does a docklands pub on a Friday night have in common," he asked, absurdly dignified, "with a bride on her wedding night?"

"The cock pit's full of bloody seamen . . ." she droned.

"Exactly!" Kendall beamed.

"And people go to this man for medicines?" Lydia whispered.

The look on Henry's face was bleak.

Outside the boarding-house, the men slid the body from the back of the cart and hoisted it onto their shoulders. George whisked the horse and cart away, while Lydia fumbled with keys retrieved from Henry's pocket.

Finally, with old George wheezing as he brought up the rear, they piled into Henry's rooms. Henry drew the curtain separating the two rooms aside, while in the dissection room, the roll of blanket hit the tabletop with a thud. Henry set lamps at each end of the body and their hazy glow made the dissection room look warm and inviting from the blackness of the studio. Lydia reached up to her earlobe and fingered the pearl set there as she followed the men into the other room and stood at Henry's shoulder.

"Now, if you recall, gentlemen, tonight we shall complete our study of the digestive tract," Henry said, bringing a stool out from under the table and offering it to Lydia.

"Don't you think she might be rather too delicate to attend, Shadwell?" Kendall asked, waving the back of his hand at Lydia.

"I believe she will survive," Lydia replied primly, perching on the stool and crossing her legs at the knee.

"If we can get past the subject of Lydia, gentlemen, so I might continue?"

Kendall raised an eyebrow at his colleague, but was quelled by a look from Henry. He offered one of the small knives to Robert. "Robert, if you'd be so kind?"

Lydia held her breath, pulling back from the table as Robert laid a careful hand on the ash-grey flesh of Cutts's naked throat. He hesitated.

"It's daft, I know," he said softly, turning to his father. "You've told me enough about him for me to know that this is what he deserves, but now I feel like I'm half as bad myself."

George nodded sympathetically. "I know, lad. But we've done worse—at least this 'un had it coming."

Robert nodded and chewed his lip. Pulling the skin taut with his fingers, he traced a neat line from the dead man's Adam's apple down the front of his body, parting layers of limp skin, spongy tissue and leathery muscle.

"What's the matter?" Henry's warm breath on Lydia's neck made her jump. She hadn't realized he'd been watching her.

"It's not bleeding," she whispered back.

"Most of the blood congeals, and fluid matter leaks away from the corpse in the hours following death," he explained. "Some passes out of the orifices."

"Orifices?"

"Holes in the body," Henry said pointedly.

"Ah." Lydia clenched the muscles in her thighs, and straightened her posture on the stool.

On the table, the two sides of the body hung open like a split fruit. Inside, a medley of bruise-like blues, purples and blacks; like spoiled meat.

"Now," Henry was saying, holding a lamp aloft to better illuminate the body, "if we can identify the path of the oesophagus and follow it down to the stomach, we'll continue our dissection there . . ."


Later, as the men piled the detached innards back into the hollowed-out torso, Lydia scooped water out of a barrel in the corner of the dissection room and set the basin on the table in front of Henry. His hands were smeared with a coppery-yellow fluid that stank like a gutter outside a butcher's shop, and she'd be damned if she'd let him touch her like that. When Henry submerged his hands in the bowl, the water turned brown.

"D'you want us to take it with us?" Robert asked, indicating the gutted corpse. Kendall had left as soon as they had finished, and Gerard was pulling on his overcoat.

"Not yet, I'll take a few samples. If you could pick it up tomorrow I'd be much obliged."

"We'll drop by tomorrow night, then," George said. "Come on, lad, let's go." At the threshold, he turned back and looked at Henry. "Thank you for the lesson."

Henry dipped his head. "You're welcome, George."

After the students had left, Henry started to clean the dirty tools left over from the dissection.

"It's Kendall, isn't it?" Lydia asked, as Henry looked up at her in surprise. "He's the one who forced you to do this."

Henry carefully wiped the keen edge of one of his knives on an old rag.

"Yes," he admitted. "Now that we have completed the digestive tract, we have only the female reproductive system to study." He set the knife down and reached for the last soiled cleaver. "Then the lessons will be at an end."

"So no more dealings with the students, then?"

"No. George persuaded Kendall to agree to that

much—once I finish the lessons, we will all go our separate ways. It's sad, really." Having finished cleaning his tools, Henry started to pack them away. "I never expected things to go sour like this."

Privately, Lydia thought that anyone could tell that a man like Kendall would be trouble.

"You forgot this," she said, grabbing a long steel implement from one of the shelves.

Henry laughed. "That wasn't used tonight—what exactly would we have done with it?"

Shrugging, she dropped the thing onto the table with a clatter. "I don't know, do I? What's it do?"

"Ah yes, you've never been pulled in for examination, have you?" Henry picked up the long, smooth, truncheon-shaped piece of metal and held it in front of Lydia's face, one eyebrow arched pointedly. Then he squeezed the end of it, and the tool expanded sideways, springing outwards.

"And you've used that thing?" Lydia said, realizing what it was. Her insides ached at the thought of being invaded by the cold metal.

"Don't look so appalled! There are medical men who claim that some women feign symptoms in order to be examined with such tools, you know."

"You're having me on."

Henry cast the terrible contraption aside. "I assure you I'm not. The speculum"—he nodded towards the shiny length of metal on the table—"was originally developed for use with prostitutes."

Lydia's jaw tightened. "I was forgetting about that. Your lot reckon us whores are born peculiar, don't they?"

"Well, yes, some of them do. It's the enquiring nature of science gone a little awry, I believe: they can't understand why some women become prostitutes and others don't, and so they assume that there must be an essential difference. A lazy assumption, in my view, and a most unscientific one."

Curiosity got the better of Lydia. "So how exactly do they think we're so different from their precious wives and daughters?"

"The belief is that women who enter prostitution have an abnormally high carnal urge: that they are addicted to a man's body, if you will, as some become addicted to spirits or opium."

Lydia's laughter filled the room, while Henry chuckled and hushed her.

"Sssh! You'll wake half of Preston!"

"So we're humping all comers because we can't think of anything nicer, that's basically it, is it?"

"Nymphomania, it's called, or sometimes andromania. There are plenty of other terms, too—it's a subject that attracts no shortage of discussion."

"Andromania." Lydia tried the strange word out.

"It's Greek. It means man-mad, loosely translated."

Lydia pursed her lips. "You'd have to be, wouldn't you?" She looked across again at the disembowelled form on the table. "You're a strange one, Henry Shadwell."

He smiled and handed her a tight roll of paper money, hugging her amiably around the waist with one arm. "Come along, I'll walk back with you. You'll never get a cab at this hour, and I don't want you out alone; you'll end up being the next on the table."

Back at Kathleen's, Lydia stumbled upstairs in the dark and stripped off the horrid black dress. Clutching the money in her hand, she flicked through, counting it—there was twice the amount Henry had promised Kathleen here. She peeled off the extra and pulled her favourite burgundy dress from her clothes chest, but paused as she realized that the bulge in the pocket was becoming rather noticeable. As an afterthought, she fished an old blood rag out from the bottom of the box and tied the money into it, before wrapping it in her old grey smock. Stuffing it in among her writing papers, she jumped into bed and lay watching the silver light of the moon until she fell asleep.

*11*

The next day, Christmas Eve, Kathleen sent Lydia and Mary to the Old Bull for dinner. Since Annabel's departure the household frequently ran out of food, and Kathleen was still struggling to find a new maid to take on Annie's tasks. The lunchtime crowds jostled around the girls as they waited for the new barmaid to bring the bubble-and-squeak Kathleen had gone in and ordered earlier in the day. Lydia's mouth watered, and she realized that she hadn't eaten anything the day before. Her paper was still waiting to be delivered to Stan the Frenchman, too, but she had not brought it out with her today. She didn't feel ready to face Mary's taunts, however good-natured and so, for now, *The White Flowers Reader* would be Lydia's secret.

"So what did your surgeon have you doing yesterday, then?" Mary teased.

Lydia knocked Mary's elbow gently with her own.

"I keep wondering what I'm going to find out about him next." She hesitated, before deciding to ask the question she'd been wanting to ask all day. "Here, have you ever had one . . . you know . . . put his mouth down there, like?" She flicked her gaze down her skirt, and looked back up at Mary, whose sapphire eyes were twinkling with undisguised mirth.

"You're telling me you've only just had one go French on you? You're pulling my leg!"

"Keep your voice down, will you? No, I'm not pulling your leg."

"I must remember to thank Mr. Shadwell on your behalf next time I see him."

"You dare. Oh, where the hell's she got to with the grub?"

Mary raised a hand in greeting as she spotted Matty across the crowded taproom.

"Hello, love," she said, as he pushed through the throng and joined them at the bar.

"Hello to you, too," he replied, pulling her to him for a kiss.

"Not staying, I'm afraid," Mary said, breaking off. "Kathleen wants us back at the house; we're just out getting dinner." The barmaid set the plates on the wooden bar with a bang, and Mary reached into the pocket of her dress for the money Kathleen had given her.

"I'll get 'em, don't worry," Matty interrupted, rummaging in his pocket and retrieving a gold sovereign.

"Lord, who's been giving you sovereigns?" Lydia asked incredulously.

"Gift from a relative, that's all. Ah, wait a minute." Digging into his pocket, Matty retrieved a handful of loose coins. Plucking the sovereign from the barmaid's fingers, he counted the money into her hand. "There you go, love."

When they got outside, Mary cuffed Matty around the ear.

"Steady on, I'm not a paying customer."

"You can say that again—look at your fingers! At least clean yourself up properly if you're going to try that on! You're just lucky we got the new girl. Alice could've been watching and all—any of the others in the Bull would've known what you were doing straight away."

Matty inspected his hands, and Lydia craned her neck to see. Sure enough, the pads of his fingers were streaked with powdery white clay from the coin-moulds he had made to cast his pewter spoons into false coin: coins he had paid with in the Bull after he had distracted the new barmaid with genuine gold.

"I thought I got it all."

"You're just getting lazy, and cocky to boot. It was

one thing when you just did strangers passing through, but around here everyone knows what you are."

"All right, all right! God, buy a girl something to eat and this is what you get. I have to keep a steady stream of business, don't I, and I'm not going to leave Preston to do it." He smiled softly at Mary, taking her hand in his. "Not before I can afford to take you with me."

"Excuse me, sir?" A beggar was shuffling towards them and beaming at Matty. Lydia wondered if he truly believed that the skinny scruffbag in front of him could be considered a "sir."

"You wouldn't consider buying a cripple a drink for Christmas, would you? One who can't work for his own?" He thrust a scabrous arm into Matty's face, and Mary wrinkled her nose at the sight of his oozing wounds. The beggar blinked pathetically at each of the girls, and smiled at Lydia.

"I'm sure you're as kind as you're pretty, a lady like you."

Lydia glanced down at her pinned-up hem, stared the man in the eye and laughed coldly. He pushed his foul arm closer to her face, and she caught a whiff of something. A familiar smell, and not one she'd have associated with dripping pus. Catching hold of his wrist, she scrutinized the marks on his arm, before scraping her fingernails across the skin. The "sores" came away, caking her nails. She sniffed her fingers, and held them under Mary's nose.

"Soap," said Mary.

The beggar's smile had faded. Slowly, deliberately, Lydia wiped the mess of melted soap and pig blood across the front of his ragged jacket.

"Clear off," she snapped. The beggar hastened away.

"Mary's right," Lydia said, turning to Matty, "you can't fool folk for ever. Someone'll catch on, and you'll be out of your depth before you know it."

On afternoons like this, Lydia could almost grow fond of Kathleen Tanner. The abbess was a formidable woman, afraid of no one and ruling her house like a queen, but as she sat with the girls in the empty parlour, munching bubble-and-squeak and refilling their cups again and again with coffee, it occurred to Lydia that she had no memories of anything like this with her mother, Nell. Kathleen knew the whore's life well, and she'd often said that there was no other way a girl like herself would have made the money for a house like this.

Last night, Lydia had mentally counted her savings again and again until sleep came, and slowly, she was starting to see the idea of a home of her own as a real possibility, rather than merely an unreachable dream. Surely Kathleen must have had these thoughts too, back when she first got a fancy for the abbess's life instead of the whore's.

"Would you believe we met a scaldrum dodger out-side the Bull?" Mary was saying.

"That right?"

Mary nodded, her reply muffled by a mouthful of food.

"I haven't seen anyone trying that around here for a while," Kathleen said.

"Came right up to me and Lydia and started showing us these sores on his arms."

Lydia nodded, ignoring her friend's omission of Matty from the story. A few months back, when rumours had first started to spread about Mistress Birch and the coiner, things had been extremely tense in the house. Kathleen was appalled by the idea that any man could have one of her girls for free, and so now, as far as she was concerned, Mary's flirtation was over. Fortunately, Kathleen didn't go out much, preferring to keep an eye on things around the house whenever possible.

"Not real sores," Lydia added. "He'd made 'em with blood and soap."

Kathleen laughed and sighed. "Whatever happened to the days when if you wanted to fleece folk, you at least had the decency to put some proper cuts in your hands? Ah, I don't know. Quiet this afternoon, isn't it?"

"It's Christmas Eve, Kathleen," Mary said. "If we get any at all, they'll come after church so their consciences are clear."

"So it is." Kathleen gasped. "Damn, I've been so busy trying to find a housemaid I forgot to get a goose."

"So it'll be soup and bacon tomorrow, then?" Lydia asked. Her stomach curdled at the thought. The bacon was always underdone when Kathleen was cooking, putting Lydia in mind of the raw bacon she would sometimes see in the workhouse yard after the rats had been making a nuisance of themselves and the warden ordered poisoned bait to be laid down. Rather than go to the trouble of visiting the chemist and signing the register for a bottle of arsenic, he'd buy arsenic-laced flypapers instead and get the inmates to soak the poison off them. Nell had done it a few times—Lydia could remember even now, because she'd always joked about flypapers being enough to kill anything if you knew what you were doing. Once, Lydia had reached for a piece of bacon she'd found in the yard, and Nell had smacked it out of her hands and clouted her around the head. *Any fool knows that's not for eating.*

"Unless one of you goes out now." Kathleen's voice stirred Lydia from her memories. "Not both, mind; I want one girl here in case we get a visitor." The abbess exhaled thoughtfully. "I really should get a new lass in, y'know. We can't go on with just the two of you for months on end, and Daisy might be a mess by the time they let her out. Some of them locked wards are rough." The room fell quiet.

"I'll go," Lydia offered, relieved to have a chance to break the silence. But she slipped back upstairs first, and tucked her five handwritten pages—three of her best stories and some notes on girls she knew in the trade—into the folds of her shawl.

She succeeded in finding a goose in the second butcher's shop she visited after dropping her writing off at the printworks. A good-sized bird, too, considering only three of them would be eating. That led to thoughts of Daisy, who had been imprisoned in the hospital for a month now. Already there were days when it was as though she had never existed, and Lydia wondered how she would be when she came out.

Leaving the butcher's, she pushed her way through the crowds of shoppers and headed down the street in search of some vegetables. There were no greens or carrots to be seen, but she did eventually manage to grab the last handful of potatoes from a barrow.

Stopping only to buy a few almond cakes that took her fancy, she headed back to Kathleen's as a fresh coating of snow began to fall.

When she turned the corner, she spotted a familiar outline: the dark, sturdy shape of Henry in his thick winter clothes. He raised a hand to reach for the doorknocker, and Lydia whistled quickly through her front teeth before he could do so.

"Ah, there you are," he said as she hurried closer. "What are you doing out in this weather?"

"Shopping for dinner." She hoisted the basket higher on her arm. "We forgot to get the goose; nobody remembers these things now Annie's gone."

Henry laughed. "I'd have got one for you. Do you have enough there?"

"It'll do fine. We haven't got any greens, though—they'd sold out."

Henry pursed his lips. "I can't give you greens, but I do have some chestnuts. I'll drop by with them later, if you like."

"Won't you be wanting them?"

Henry's gaze shifted almost imperceptibly from Lydia's eyes to her cheek. "No. I have a dinner invitation tomorrow, so I shan't be at home to eat them."

"Anywhere nice?"

"Oh . . . you know. Anyway, the chestnuts are yours if you'd like them."

Lydia smiled. "That's good of you."

Henry shifted slightly. "The reason I came by was to tell you that I've just received a message from Mr. Hollingworth's house: it seems one of his daughters is very sick. They called a physician out to her and he has diagnosed tuberculosis—consumption, you know—but he needs a surgeon to clear her chest. I'll check on your sister if I possibly can, not that I imagine we'll have any time to chat."

"You're too kind to me, Henry." With a shifty glance at the parlour window, Lydia reached up on tiptoes and kissed his cheek. Grunting slightly under his breath, Henry caught hold of her chin and kissed her on the lips, licking a snowflake from the corner of her mouth.

"Annie won't get consumption, too, will she?"

"It's unlikely. They'll have maids nursing the child."

"What about you?"

"I won't be there long, and in any case, I'm accustomed to protecting myself from infection."

"Can't I go with you? I'll wait outside."

"It's better if you stay here. I have to go now, but I'll tell you what I know when I bring those chestnuts."

She watched as he walked up the street and turned back onto Fishergate. Something felt wrong, and she couldn't shake the feeling that, deep down, she knew what that thing was.

As Mary had predicted, the house was quiet until the congregations started to spill out of the local churches. Apart from a few moments to greet each man, Kathleen busied herself in the kitchen, pulling the giblets from the goose and doing her best to butter its skin. Lydia had briefly gone into the kitchen for a cup of ale, but found she couldn't stay—the memory of Henry's anatomy lesson was too fresh in her mind.

Back in the parlour, Mary was regarding a dully dressed

man (a Methodist, Lydia decided) with a familiar expression of disdain that Lydia still found amusing.

"Been out somewhere respectable?" she sneered. Lydia swallowed a giggle.

"I—I've been to church."

"And now you're done being holy, and you want to come and dirty my sheets?"

"I won't dirty them, miss, I promise."

"Like I haven't heard that before. Now get upstairs before you really try my patience."

The man shuffled out into the hall, and Mary followed, pausing only momentarily to wink at Lydia over her shoulder.

The next chap arrived while they were still upstairs, and was soon in Lydia's room. He pushed her down on her back, and she watched him closely from under her eyelashes. Not too old, not too bad-looking, yet she'd never seen him before. She came to the conclusion that this wasn't a regular habit for him—probably more like a Christmas treat he'd given himself. Her mind wandered as she thought of Henry and Annie, and she hoped she wouldn't be trapped upstairs when Henry returned.

As the man left, Lydia could hear that Mary was still busy across the landing. Sitting up on the windowsill, she watched the street below, her eyes flitting across the windows of the houses until she found one with light shining through the glass. Warm, safe, inviting. Perhaps when she had a home of her own, she could persuade Annie to leave her governess job—maybe Mary and Matty would move in, too, if there was enough space, and Daisy might want to come, when she left the hospital . . . Oh, now she was just being silly. Lydia pushed the thought from her mind.

The sound of footsteps on the stairs told her that the shame-faced Methodist had finally fled. Lydia joined Mary on the landing, and they sauntered downstairs together.

"I wish you wouldn't keep grinning at me like that!" Mary chuckled.

"I can't help it. When you start that act I can't keep a straight face. That stuff about holiness, where d'you come up with it?"

"A priest back when I was a girl in Ireland. He used to bawl at us, talking about how we had to repent or go to Hell and burn." Mary smiled, but it was an awkward smile that soon faded, and Lydia pursed her lips.

"D'you think we are going to Hell, then?"

Mary shrugged. "Perhaps. I s'pose I do still think that. I've been told how to get to Heaven since the day I was born, but I've ignored every word."

Lydia was with another man—little more than a lad, really—when she heard the doorbell ring. She strained to hear over the rasping, hesitant sound of his breath as

Kathleen opened the door downstairs. Lydia tried not to look irritated as she struggled to follow the faint sound of conversation drifting up from the hall. There it was—the smooth tone of Henry's voice. The lad on top of her didn't look anywhere close to finishing. She wriggled underneath him, made satisfied noises, squeezed him as tightly as she could; nothing worked.

"I'm sorry," he muttered, rolling off her, "you're probably not used to this."

Lydia forced a smile. "More used to it than you might think. Anything I can do?"

"No, not really. I wouldn't dream of coming here normally. Sorry, that probably sounded rather insulting." He laughed nervously.

"I've had worse said to me." Lydia sighed. She could still hear Henry downstairs.

"This . . . this was my father's idea. I think he's with your friend. Did I say the right thing there—is she your friend?"

"Who, Mary? Aye, we're friends. Anyhow, there must be something we can do. Have you never done this before?"

The lad was silent.

"Come on, cat got your tongue? Never been with a girl?"

"Yes, of course!" He drew himself up in absurd indignation, then appeared to lose heart. "No. No, I've never been with a girl."

Nodding, Lydia smoothed her skirts down. "I see. Look, how's about we forget about this? Your father don't have to know any different so long as I get paid as normal." Kathleen was still talking to someone in the hall. Perhaps Lydia would have time to speak to Henry after all.

"Really?" Now the young man looked nervous, studying Lydia as if she were a page of some strange foreign script.

"Really. I just want my money."

"That's good of you." He fussed about for a few minutes, finding Lydia's money and fiddling with his shirtsleeves, while she sat on the bed and forced herself not to usher him out. Just as she felt ready to scream in frustration, he muttered a few more apologies and thanks and made his way out. Before he had left, though, she heard the front door close downstairs.

"Was that Henry?" Still dishevelled, she had run down to the kitchen as soon as the lad was safely out of the way. Kathleen, on her knees in front of the stove, blinked in surprise.

"Yes, he was dropping off some chestnuts. You done already?"

Lydia chuckled. "Nowt to finish doing. I reckon that lad's pa will be waiting till the last trumpet if he wants any grandchildren, though."

Kathleen grunted and returned her attention to the stove.

"Did Henry have any news?"

"News? No." The abbess eyed Lydia. "Are you *sure* there's nothing going on between you two?"

"If there was I'd hardly expect him to speak to you about it, would I?"

"You're a secretive little slut these days. What 'news' were you expecting?"

"It's about Annie, if you must know! He's been to pay a visit to one of the children she teaches: the girl's sick."

"Is that right?"

Lydia groaned. Her eyes felt hot. "Yes! Kathleen, I am not about to run off and marry Henry Shadwell!"

The abbess sighed and wiped the soot from her hands onto a dishrag. She had finally managed to light the stove, and the flames licked hungrily at the dry wood inside.

Christmas Day was as quiet as it had been on Lydia's first Christmas at the house a year ago. Daisy had told her back then that they rarely got any business during the day—the men were all off having dinner with their families—but they sometimes got one or two at night, those who could nip out for an hour or two. Much to Lydia's surprise, Mary gave her a gift of a gold-coloured ring; she in turn improvised by giving Mary one of the almond cakes she had bought at the market the day before.

Turning the ring on her finger, she whispered, "Is this one of Matty's that turn your fingers green?"

"No, I got it off a cheap-jack: the one you got your little crown brooch from. Matty's sold all his rings now; he'll have to get more."

"He's not sold any of 'em to people around here, has he?" Matty's cockiness in handing his pewter coins to the Bull's barmaid had worried both girls, and the locals would know where to find him when their fingers turned green and they discovered the truth about his "gold" rings.

Mary exhaled gloomily. "He says not. I'm never sure if he's telling the truth, though."

"Did he get you anything?"

"Aye, this." Mary reached deep into the bodice of her dress and fished out a gold locket on a long chain. She snapped it open, but it was empty.

"Aren't you supposed to have a picture or a lock of hair in there?" Lydia asked, taking hold of the dangling locket and turning it over. The back of the piece was slightly uneven, and she ran her thumb over it.

"Give me a chance! I must remember to ask Matty for some of his hair when I see him next."

"Hmm. Here, it's rough on the back."

Mary nodded, closing the locket and scooping it back inside her dress as the sound of Kathleen moving about in the next room drew closer.

"He just heats it a bit over a candle so he can get rid of any engravings."

"He's handling stolen property now?" Lydia whispered incredulously. Mary shifted awkwardly; more, Lydia suspected, out of fear at the thought of what would happen to her beau if he was nabbed than from any prickling of her conscience.

"I know," she said softly, "but I don't think he makes a habit of it. He just saw someone selling this and knew I'd love it. He keeps telling me that no girl's ever trusted him like I do, even though I know all about what he gets up to. Said I deserved something special for Christmas."

Lydia was silent, but her hand drifted up under her hair to finger one of the pearls Henry had given her.

"Here you go." Kathleen emerged from the kitchen with a brandy bottle and sloshed generous measures into glasses for the girls. "You can have a little of the strong stuff today."

Behind her tilted glass, Mary shot Lydia a wide-eyed look of surprise.

"Oh—and I have something else, too." Kathleen lifted the lid of one of the parlour's padded footstools. "I saw these and thought they'd suit you." She handed the girls a dress each: Lydia's dusky pink and Mary's sky blue. As Lydia took hers by its shoulders and shook it out, a matching pair of ruffled drawers and two new pairs of stockings tumbled from the folds. She looked at Mary, startled.

"And they'll do for working, too, of course." Kathleen's guarded smile had returned. "I get my money back in the end."

Lydia laughed and planted a kiss on Kathleen's cheek, before she could protest. Mary kissed the other side of the abbess's face.

"Oh, stop it—I shan't get you anything else if you come over all daft." Kathleen wiped her face with the back of her hand. "Kippers, anyone?"


All day, Lydia had to remind herself that Henry would not be coming round—he had told her he had an invitation to spend Christmas elsewhere, though he had not said where, and Lydia couldn't find the words to ask him. *What's the matter with you, you stupid tart?* she scolded herself. As the lazy Christmas afternoon passed, she grew angrier and angrier, fiddling with the pearl earrings he had given her, unable to banish Henry from her mind.

"Lydia! Dinner!" The smell of overdone goose and potatoes drifted through from the kitchen, and she slouched through to where Kathleen and Mary were just finishing setting the food out on the kitchen table—a banquet, by the house's standards. Kathleen poured cups of ale as Lydia took a seat. Grace was never said in this house—Kathleen had said in the past that she thought God would take it as a mockery, and she preferred not to rile Him more than necessary. Mary raised her cup, however.

"To Daisy," she said, "who'll be back at this table with us this time next year, God willing."

"Daisy," Lydia and Kathleen echoed. *And Annie*, Lydia added silently.

"And may I be filthy stinking rich when she gets here," Kathleen added, tipping the ale down her throat. She had fried chipolatas to go with the goose, and wrapped them in pink blankets of bacon. The memory of Jimmy from the workhouse surfaced in Lydia's mind, and she automatically pushed the sausage and bacon to the side of her plate. At once, Kathleen leaned over and speared them with her fork, dropping one onto her own plate and shoving the other in her mouth. She chewed and swallowed, then nodded at Lydia.

"Is Mr. Shadwell wanting you round at his place to-morrow, or will you be here?"

Lydia thought quickly.

"Yes—he asked me to meet him there," she lied. "I'll have to leave just after breakfast."

"I think Lydia might beat you to the riches at this rate," Mary chuckled. Her face was flushed a delicate pink from the brandy. Lydia glared at her.

"Yes, well," Kathleen said.

But at least the abbess hadn't forbidden her to go.

## 12

It wasn't easy finding a carriage for hire on Boxing Day but eventually Lydia settled herself into a shabby little conveyance driven by a man who looked like he needed the money: he was painfully thin, and despite the foul weather he wore a thin, threadbare jacket in place of a coat. It would have taken Lydia the best part of the day to walk to Henry's dockland workshop, and she didn't even know for certain that he was there. When she knocked on the rotting wooden door of his rooms, though, her shoulders slackened in relief at the sound of floorboards creaking underfoot.

"Who is it?"

"Henry, it's me."

"Lydia?" The door opened a crack, and Henry peered through the gap before opening it. "I'm sorry, did I say I'd collect you?"

"No, no. I just thought I'd come and see if you spoke to my sister."

"Ah yes, of course. Come in." Henry stepped back from the door. He had on his filthy dissecting apron, and wiped smears of foul-smelling stuff from his hands onto it. "You'll have to take me as you find me, I'm afraid."

Lydia followed him through into the dissection room, and recoiled instantly as a rank odour hit her.

"Ah, God!"

"Oh!" With an apologetic grin, Henry grabbed a glass jar that sat in the middle of the table and poured a measure of liquid into it. A ratty lump of greyish flesh that had been sitting at the bottom of the jar floated up into the middle of the container. Henry capped the jar and put it on the shelf with the others, before fanning his notes around to waft away the stink.

"Sorry about that. Just one of the samples I took from our mutual friend Mr. Cutts."

"What the hell is it?" she said, eyeing the specimen in its jar.

"The larynx."

Lydia looked at Henry, one eyebrow raised.

"It's where the vocal cords are. The organ that allows us to speak, if you will. All dead tissue smells terrible after a while," he said. "Look at these." Protruding from a wooden box in the corner of the room was a jumble of bones, with shrivelled scraps of flesh and fat still clinging to them.

"You kept his bones?"

"Yes, I'm building a skeleton for my laboratory."

Lydia eyed the box of bones. "Very decorative."

"Well, it is Christmas, I have to brighten the place up somehow." Henry grinned. "Speaking of the festive season, did you enjoy the chestnuts?"

"We all did, thank you." Lydia realized she was fingering the pearl in her ear, and dropped her hand back down to her side. "So . . . did you speak to Annie?"

"Of course. You came to ask about Annabel." Henry plucked a long bone out of the box and started scrubbing it with a stiff brush. "I did speak to her, but not at length, I'm afraid. I was being led downstairs by the nursemaid after seeing the Hollingworth child, and Annabel popped her head out of the schoolroom door. She recognized me. Of course, I couldn't really say anything about you, or ask too many questions when the nursemaid was just ahead of me, so I simply greeted her and asked if she was well."

"And what did she say?"

"She said she was, but . . ."

"What is it, Henry?"

"Well, she seemed anxious, my dear. It seemed to me there was something upsetting her."

Lydia sighed and closed her eyes, impotently wishing

the whole damned mess away. She thought of her gents' paper, waiting at Stanley Stoker's to be printed, and her nerve faltered. Was it just a fond notion to hope for a new life for herself?

When Henry spoke again, the deep tones of his voice rumbled in her ears.

"I won't lie and tell you that you're wrong to be concerned. But if it's any comfort, she doesn't look as if she's ailing in any way. I don't think you should be mortally afraid for her. Why not write to her if you're concerned? I can give you the address if you don't have it. It'll be in my black notebook in the other room."

"I'll do that. She was supposed to write to me and tell me the address, but she never did." Lydia looked away momentarily. "Thank you, Henry. So, did you enjoy your dinner?"

"I beg your pardon?"

"Your Christmas dinner. You said you had an invitation."

"Oh. Yes." Henry picked very assiduously at a sinew of flesh on the bone he was cleaning, and Lydia felt the back of her neck prickle.

"Henry?"

He plucked the scrap from the bone and flicked it onto the tabletop. "Yes, it was pleasant. Not much to tell, really—a dinner's a dinner, isn't it?"

"Friends of yours?"

"In a sense. I met them fairly recently. Now I come to

think of it, I'm going to need some new pictures of you—that is, if you don't mind?"

"No, I don't mind. Why didn't you say something sooner?"

"I've been busy. It slipped my mind. My customers are clamouring for new stock; you're a popular subject, it seems. We'll have to hurry, though: I'll be busy tonight." He paused, looking at Lydia. "I'm collecting a few bodies from the workhouse. Hopefully there will be a suitable one so that I can complete my lessons."

Lydia was silent, flicking back through her memories like the pages of an old book. The great hulking mass of the workhouse, the yard that was always painfully cold in winter and scorching in summer, the rows of narrow beds, like graves in the cemetery. And Jimmy, poor Jimmy. She hadn't been anywhere near the Union Workhouse in years—Nell had seemed to have a superstitious fear that someone would run out and haul them back in if they passed too close. Her throat felt dry and parched, and she swallowed reflexively.

"I'm coming with you," she said. Henry stared at her.

"I beg your pardon?"

"Tonight, when you go to the workhouse. I'm coming with you." She didn't want to end up like Nell, afraid even to walk within the building's shadow; and more than that, she feared her courage failing her when the time came to collect her papers. It was her only chance, and if she had to remind herself of the hell she came from, then so be it.

"I left the workhouse when I was little more than a babby," she said eventually. "Your bodies aren't likely to be anyone I know."

"Very well." Henry nodded, smiling hesitantly. Sometimes the way he looked at Lydia was unsettling, as if she were teetering on the brink of lunacy and had to be treated with care. "You know, I haven't eaten and we've got a busy day ahead: would you like to go to an alehouse for lunch, after we've taken the photographs? Consider it another Christmas gift."

Lydia stood quietly, watching Henry. Of course he was uncomfortable—any idiot could see that—but why?

"Lydia?"

She forced a smile. "No. I mean, yes. That'd be nice."

"Good," Henry said, nodding decisively. He tossed the bone back into the box. "I'll clean myself up."

The place he took her to was one she hadn't visited before: a large, whitewashed pub at the top of the hill on Friargate. Their footsteps echoed on the scarred wooden floor as they walked in, and the barmaid looked up from polishing a tankard.

"Afternoon," she said cheerily.

They shared a pitcher of ale and a large kidney pie, bigger than the plate it came on and oozing gravy.

"Henry," Lydia asked, licking pastry crumbs from her lips, "where do you live?"

"Excuse me?"

"Well, I know you don't live at your workshop." Although she had no intention of admitting it to Henry, she had even tried looking on the silver tray in the parlour where Kathleen kept all the useful cards she was given, but Henry's had not been among them. Knowing Kathleen, Lydia doubted that the abbess would have thrown away the card of a nearby surgeon, even if she didn't always trust him. Far more likely that she would hide it from Lydia's prying eyes.

He picked a sliver of gristle from his pie with a fork, and wiped it off the prongs onto the side of the plate. "I was in rented rooms until recently. I've just bought my first house."

"So is it the surgeon's wage that paid for the place, or should you be thanking a certain young lady?" She grinned, but Henry's smile was hesitant. Her heart thumped in her chest.

"I suppose so."

"It's all right for some," she said. "I pose for the pictures, but it's you that gets a new house."

"You mean you're looking for a place of your own, Lydia?"

Her hesitation answered his question, and she realized that she had made her mind up.

"I . . ." The words died on her lips, and she was afraid he would laugh.

"I didn't realize. I don't mean to be rude, but how do you expect to pay for a home of your own?"

Over the past year, Lydia had developed a habit of holding her breath and curling her tongue tightly whenever she knew that it would be safer to take the time to think before she spoke. She did so now, and Henry waited in silence for her to continue.

"I have plans." A minute ago, she might have told Henry about her intention to go ahead with her smut-writing, with or without his help, but the fact that he'd obviously forgotten their earlier conversation on the subject nettled her. Her hands felt twitchy, and she took up her fork and started poking the leftover piecrust to bits.

"Plans?" Henry was looking at her with interest now, and she waited for him to catch onto her train of thought.

"I've been saving, and I've got some other ideas." The crust was down to crumbs now.

"You're being very evasive today."

"Evasive?"

"Secretive."

"Ha!" Gritting her teeth and biting back a sharp retort,

Lydia merely glared at him. His black-brown eyes faltered, and he looked down at his plate.

"I understand. We all have our personal business."

Lydia reached out across the tabletop and touched the tips of Henry's fingers with her own. "Henry . . ."

His little finger flickered slightly, caressing her nails.

"Lydia, I know I've asked a lot from you, and I see now that I haven't given you much in return. I owe you more than that."

At the bar, a handful of men were waiting for their drinks. One of them looked across to where the well-dressed man sat, hesitantly handclasped with a prostitute. Lydia lowered her gaze and studied the tiny dark hairs on the back of Henry's hand, remembering Kathleen's warning that Henry would never forget that theirs was a business relationship.

"If you have plans for a new life," Henry was saying, "I would like to help."

She nodded. "If I need your help, I'll ask. How's that?"

"That sounds fine. It's the least I can do."


After Henry had hailed a cab to take him back to his workshop and his box of bones, Lydia walked back down Friargate towards the centre of town. Boxing Day had kept the quality at home and the streets were quieter than usual, occupied only by vagabonds and servants shopping for perishables. On an impulse, she turned right instead of left and walked down to where the shops on Fishergate gave way to the train station and rows of tall red brick houses. She scrutinized a couple of the curtained windows, to assess which were private residences and which offered rooms for rent, but the blank white lace behind the glass gave nothing away. She turned back, vowing to buy herself a newspaper the next day and scour the notices.

Back at the introduction house, she slammed the door on the brutal wind that had chased her all the way back. Kicking her boots against the brass shoe cleaner in the hall, she threw her shawl off with a shiver.

"Lydia? That you? Come in here for a minute."

Her stomach lurched as she made her way through to the kitchen.

She needn't have worried. Standing by the fire with Kathleen and Mary was a rosy blonde with high cheekbones and her hair twisted up in a knot that was threatening to fall out.

"Lydia, this is Connie, the new maid."

So Kathleen had finally found a servant girl who'd work in a place like this. Kathleen must have given Connie an outline of her duties by now, but the girl looked as though she couldn't have asked for a better Christmas present.

"Er, hello," Lydia said.

Connie merely grinned like a simpleton. Lydia forced a smile.

Mary gestured to Lydia and led her out into the parlour. As the door closed behind them, Lydia pressed her fingers against her mouth to stifle a giggle, and stared at her friend in disbelief.

"Where the hell did she find that Connie, then?"

"I've no idea, she just came back with her. I s'pose beggars can't be choosers, and there's not a lot of girls who'd work here, is there? So, what immoral acts has your Mr. Shadwell had you committing today, then?"

"He took me for dinner, as it happens."

"Oh, shame."

Lydia flopped down into one of the parlour armchairs, trying not to stare too closely at the pile of gents' papers on the table. "He's picking me up again tonight."

Mary nodded. "Got some stamina, that surgeon of yours."

Dusk was falling when Lydia made her way back down to the parlour after servicing her fourth man of the afternoon. Mary was sprawled in one of the chairs with her boots up on the polished tabletop. Immediately Lydia's thoughts turned to her sister: Annabel would not have hesitated to berate Mary for such behaviour. Lydia resolved to write a letter that evening, before Henry collected her to take her to the workhouse.

"All right there, you dirty old tart?" Mary grinned mischievously at Lydia, who stuck two fingers up at her. In the corner, Connie looked up from dusting Kathleen's collection of pottery and laughed loudly, causing Lydia and Mary to jump as one.

"This place is so much better than my last," the housemaid trilled. There was something insincere about her voice: a forced airiness that set Lydia's teeth on edge. "Lord, they were stiff old sods."

"Connie, I'm going to have to ask—I can't help myself," Lydia said, peeling the paper wrapping off a chocolate from a box left by one of Mary's besotted slaves. "What made you want to work in a house like this?" She arched an eyebrow at Mary. Kathleen might kill them for it, but maybe they could get rid of this one before her voice and her laugh sent them all barmy.

Connie looked surprised that the question had even been asked. "It's so much more relaxed here," she protested. "Going into service anywhere else is just so *dull*. I want the pretty clothes and the white sheets like you've got here. And you don't have to bob about, curtsying to everyone."

"But you're in the attic room, and you still have a pallet with cheap sheets there. You're the housemaid, Connie, not one of the girls."

"Not yet." The maid smiled coyly, and Mary sat up straight in her chair.

"What d'you mean, 'not yet?'"

"Oh, nothing, nothing! I just mean that when I've been here a few weeks and your abbess sees how well I work, she might reconsider, that's all."

"If Kathleen had wanted to hire you as a whore, she'd have said so," Mary warned. "She won't take any shit off you."

Lydia nodded. "A word to the wise, Connie: if you want to start out in the trade, don't do it by getting on the wrong side of Kathleen. She's been in this game a long time, and she knows everyone."

"And if you go behind her back, they'll all know about it."

Connie didn't seem to have heard them. "And of course, the blokes what can afford it like to keep a girl to themselves; less chance of catching something nasty." Lydia and Mary turned as one to glare at her. "That's the sweetest living, I reckon," she continued regardless, "being a kept mistress." Finally putting down the vase she'd been slapping with the duster, Connie smiled at the girls. "Have neither of you had the chance to do that?"

"And turned 'em all down, thank you kindly," Lydia scoffed. "A mistress's job is all the fuss and danger of a whore's and a wife's rolled up together." She turned to Mary. "That reminds me; did you hear about Betsy Ward? Died having whatshisname's baby just last week."

Betsy Ward had worked for one of the other Preston houses, until her best customer decided he wanted her to himself. Despite the large release fee Betsy's abbess would have received, Kathleen had been thrilled to hear that her rival had lost one of her best girls.

"Can't say I'm surprised. She was fucking huge when she was in the Bull last, and only seven months gone. I thought then it might split her in half."

"So you don't have favourites, then?" Connie interrupted. "Or sweethearts, nothing like that?"

Mary shook her head, but said nothing.

"No," said Lydia firmly. "Neither of us have."

# 13

The mourning weeds were as tight and itchy as Lydia had remembered them, and she swore under her breath as she and Henry sat huddled in the open back of George's cart. As George's horse pulled the cart uphill, she saw it at once—the ominous shadow with its central tower. She thought she'd forgotten the place, but it all came back to her now. George drove the cart to the back of the building, and Lydia strained to look in through the windows, but all was black inside. No sense being up once it was too dark to work.

"Right," Henry said, hopping down from the back of the cart, "the mortuary is in an outbuilding behind the ward, so we'll have to go through that way. Were you ever in the hospital wing?"

"Only when I was born," Lydia replied dryly. She had forgotten her gloves, and her hands were balled into fists to keep out the cold. Henry snatched up Lydia's bare hands in his gloved ones and squeezed them.

"Come on. It doesn't usually take long."

Henry's gentle tap on the side door was answered by a hulking brute of a night watchman with broken teeth and a shorn head, terrier-cropped like a convict. Nodding to Henry in greeting, he ushered them in, looking askance at Lydia from underneath large, uneven eyebrows.

"Lydia is a friend of mine," Henry explained. "She won't be in the way: she can wait in the hospital wing while we go out to the mortuary."

The watchman shrugged. "If you like. I wouldn't take any of the women in my family in there, mind. There's more than colds gets passed around in here."

"I'm standing in the same room as them, not fucking them," Lydia snapped, "and d'you think I could get on with it, please?"

Henry winked at her, and the startled man threw the infirmary door open, muttering something about young lasses these days. The three of them slipped into the darkened corridor of the hospital wing.

"We're just going to nip through there," Henry said in an undertone, indicating a nearby door. "That's the night watchman's room, and the door in there opens out onto the yard, so we can get to the mortuary without being seen by any of the inmates. We won't be long." Then he was gone, ducking through the door of the office after the giant watchman, and Lydia was left alone.

At once, she felt fidgety, and couldn't keep still. She rubbed her cold hands together, then paced up and down the corridor. As she walked further, she spied an open door: the workhouse ward, known to the inmates as "the sickhouse." She looked back over her shoulder. Henry had still not returned. Her feet no longer felt like her own as she stepped through into the ward, the room in which she had been born.

It was dark and quiet, all the inmates laid out in rows in their worn old beds. Lydia watched the slumbering mounds as she crept past, trying to minimize the echo of her boots on the bare floor. A gurgle from a phlegmy inmate made her jump, and she pressed her hands to her mouth to stop herself from crying out.

A watery moonbeam shone through the very tops of the arched windows, lending the ward a faint, milky light that slowly allowed her to pick out the movements of the sleeping patients in their beds. At least one of them, she suspected, would not move for much longer— the blanket covering the gaunt young woman in the bed closest to her heaved irregularly with the sharp, useless breaths of the dying. Lydia shifted further down the wall, and the moonlight caught the glassy surfaces of the girl's eyes, staring without sight at Lydia as her blue-lipped mouth gaped like a netted fish's. Across the room, the rasp of someone clearing their throat preceded spitting. There was, Lydia realized, a thick smell of phlegm in the air, under the acid of puke and piss. Somewhere a child was whimpering, perhaps in its sleep, perhaps not. Again came the sound of someone gobbing up, closer this time; close enough for Lydia to flinch from the smell. The rustle of straw mattresses made her think of Nell and the boarding-house, and she forced herself to study the leaded lines on the windows. Suddenly, she realized that she could no longer hear the hiss of the dying girl's breath, but couldn't be sure exactly when it had stopped. Then she heard a door banging in the distance, and she hurried back out into the corridor before Henry and the night watchman returned.

She was quiet for the duration of the journey back to the boarding-house. There were three bodies wrapped up in the back of the cart. The leap from a talking, moving, eating, fucking person and the lifeless meat in Henry's dissection room didn't seem so strange when you looked at the sick and dying workhouse inmates: gasping out their lives, ignored, reduced to bodies whose only efforts were expended in the futile struggle to hold onto life.

. . .

Henry's students had gathered in the corridor outside his rooms. Instructing Robert and Kendall to fetch the bodies from the cart, he unlocked the door and strode in, taking a lamp from his desk and lighting it. Gerard followed Henry and Lydia straight to the dissection room.

"You may wish to wait here, Lydia," Henry said. "The specimen we shall be using tonight is a woman." Lydia returned his smooth gaze and reassured him that it made no difference. But just for a moment, she trembled at the thought of those neat, skilled hands slitting her open and pulling out a handful of her guts.

"These are the ones I can't be doing with," George muttered darkly. "Butchering murderers and the likes of John Cutts I can cope with, but these poor sods . . ." He shrugged helplessly. "They were poor, that's all. It don't seem right that not having a pot to piss in leads you to the same place as if you'd strangled someone."

Lydia reached a hand out to the head of the bed to steady herself. All of a sudden, her legs felt weak, and Henry gently instructed her to sit down on the mattress.

"Will you be taking any organs or bone specimens?" Gerard called from the dissection room.

"No, not this time," Henry shouted back. "Ah, there you are." Robert and Kendall hauled the sack into Henry's rooms.

"No rest for the wicked, eh, Shadwell?"

Lydia jumped to her feet. She turned to see Henry's fellow surgeon, Thomas, standing in the doorway. Henry meanwhile had turned quite pale. Clearing his throat, he waved irritably at the men lugging the corpse.

"Just start setting up in there. I'll come through in a moment."

"Are you quite all right?" Thomas asked. Lydia stared at him, looking for any sign of the disease he'd given Daisy.

"Lydia!" Henry snapped.

"What?"

"I told you to go in the other room."

"No," she replied, stung, "you told *them* to go in the other room."

"I seem to have come at a bad time," Thomas interrupted, his eyes wide with confusion. "I'll be in Crewe visiting family over the next few days, Henry, but I heard about your news in the Old Bull this evening and I wanted to congratulate you before I left."

"Lydia, will you please excuse us for one moment?" Henry said. His voice shook ever so slightly. She planted her feet and folded her arms.

"There's no need for that, Henry," Thomas went on. "I merely came to congratulate you on your engagement."

Lydia could see Henry looking at her, but his gaze was distant, almost as though he were standing in a separate room. Thomas's footsteps were heading down the stairs, but already she couldn't remember his face. In among all the whirling confusion and anger, there was a pain in the middle of her chest: an indignant, humiliated pain that flashed brighter and hotter when Henry finally moved towards her and laid a hand on her shoulder.

"Lydia, I was going to explain—"

She brushed his hand away and pulled her cape tighter about her shoulders. The damned mourning dress was itching like a biblical plague. "I don't see why. You don't owe me the truth about yourself any more than I owe you the truth about me." Her throat tightened, and she stamped towards the door.

"Lydia, if you just wait until the students have gone, I'll—"

"I helped you with your pictures, didn't I? I helped you . . ." She tailed off, allowing the memory of the day she had scouted around the cemetery to hang silently in the air between them before continuing. "And now I'm done, for good. You never said you wanted nothing else, and there's no sense in me being here wasting time when I could be back at Kathleen's making money." She sniffed haughtily. "I won't trouble you for what you owe me, I can see you're busy. You can pay Kathleen tomorrow."

Henry stood mute in his waistcoat and shirtsleeves. Lydia waited for a moment, then turned and ran down the rotten staircase.

. . .

Her feet were blistered by the time she reached the railway station. As she withdrew from her reverie, the pain in her feet was joined by other sensations—the ragged, blood-flavoured breath of one on the verge of exhaustion, the scratching of the cheap widow's weeds, and above all, a strange humming all over her body—a threat of an all-consuming pain that threatened to swallow her whole. She sagged against the wall of the railway bridge and spat onto the tracks below. Pulling her purse from her pocket, she wrenched the mourning dress from her shoulders, sending a confetti of little buttons pattering onto the frozen ground. Letting the dress pool at her feet, she stepped out of it and limped down Fishergate, with her cloak pulled tightly around her and her purse clutched in her hand.

Outside the Bull, she halted and stood in the doorway, listening to the hum of conversation and the clinking of glasses. The scent of ale and spirits drifted from within, and with it the promise of blissful amnesia. Underneath her cloak, Lydia's fingers tightened on her purse. Then she rearranged her cloak and marched through the door.

She awoke the next morning with the white mid-morning light streaming in through her window, and the hubbub of the town drifting over from the main road. Her head throbbed, and the stale taste in her mouth added to her rising sensation of nausea. Wincing at a cramp in her hip, she straightened herself up from where she had been sleeping, slumped at the fireside in her bedroom amid a pile of papers. As she moved, an empty blue glass gin bottle toppled over and rolled across the fireplace. The fire had died down to greying embers overnight, and sooty smudges intermingled with disjointed fragments of stories and attempts at bawdy verse. She couldn't recall writing any of it. Getting up, she shook what she could of the coal dust back into the grate and tucked the papers away in her chest.

Downstairs in the kitchen, Mary flinched at the sight of her.

"Sweet Mother, what've you been doing? You look dreadful."

The abbess spun around to look at her and Lydia shot a warning glance at Mary.

"I got back late last night, that's all. I'll look fine once I've had a bite to eat and put some paint on."

"I hope you're right," Kathleen grumbled, eyeing Connie carefully as she hoisted the porridge pot off the stove. "Watch where you're going with that, girl! Lydia, you're not sickening for something, are you? You don't half look rough."

Connie clattered the saucepan in the sink, and looked somewhat alarmed.

"I'm perfectly fine!" Lydia looked across at Mary, who cleared her throat.

"I think you're fussing over nothing, Kathleen. You're just used to seeing Lydia painted up in the mornings; she always looks a fright beforehand." Reaching for the stone jar of honey, Mary drizzled the sticky amber liquid over Lydia's porridge and pushed it across the table to her. Lydia, her stomach still churning, forced spoon after spoon into her mouth—Kathleen would explode if she found out that Lydia had downed a whole bottle of blue ruin the night before. Truth be told, Lydia was furious with herself. One bottle of gin hadn't bankrupted her, true, but the knowledge that Henry's revelation had driven her to drink and caused her to spend some of her treasured savings was like a knife in her ribs.

# 14

1889

The New Year began quietly. For the first few days, Lydia stayed indoors, scribbling in her bedroom whenever she had some time alone, and hoarding away the money she earned. The tatty rag she wrapped her money in was now pleasingly fat and heavy. For a penny a time (and one free fuck at the beginning), the baker's lad would collect the money for Lydia's newspapers and bring them to her, as well as buying a stamp for the letter she'd written to ask after Annie. Now she waited for a reply, poring over the advertisements for rooms to rent whenever she had a minute to herself.

Mary tried to draw her out on the subject of Henry, convinced that Lydia was heartbroken. Unused to compassion, Lydia found herself unable to respond to Mary's concern. However strange the experience was, she appreciated it, although her affection for her friend faltered when she caught a flicker of pity in Mary's eyes.

Finally, she worked up the courage to go out into town and collect her papers. Stan had told her that they would be ready in the first week of the New Year, and Lydia scurried along Fishergate and down Glovers Court with her eyes on her boots, hoping that she would not see Henry. When she arrived at the printworks, they were waiting there for her: two hundred neat little papers, about half the size of an ordinary newspaper, with her title—*The White Flowers Reader*—emblazoned across the top in the fancy font she had picked out. She looked at Stan in silence, her hand suspended in the air over the top of the pile. She felt as if she should ask permission to touch them.

"Go on," the printer said good-naturedly. "Best to check everything's right."

She picked the top paper off the pile and flicked through each of its ten pages in turn. These were her words—the stories she had written in the privacy of her room whenever she was alone, and the thoughts she had composed on the introduction houses in the town and the girls working in them (she had taken special care to speak well of Kathleen's house, hoping that would temper the abbess's mood when she found out), and the two illustrations she had chosen from Stan's box of stock plates. She wanted to show the world, yet she was afraid of what people might say. She wondered what the lad who'd set her text out on the letterpress, letter by painstaking letter, had thought of her stories: had he enjoyed them? Had he laughed? Or had he paid attention only to the task in hand?

"If you want to leave some here, I can show them to the folk who come in here to collect fresh stock," Stan was saying. "A lot of the booksellers and the abbesses come straight to me to choose the ones they want. A few of the collectors do and all. It helps to keep things discreet, from your point of view, and I can keep an account for you so you can collect your money from here if I do sell any."

Lydia nodded, taking a handful of papers from the top of the pile. "Thank you. I'll just take a few away with me," she said, when she had found her voice. "You show the others to your regulars."

One morning, when a knock at her bedroom door had given Lydia sufficient warning to stuff her writing things under the bed and brush down her skirts, she opened her door, her mask-like smile on her face, to see Henry standing there. She froze, her hand gripping the doorframe.

"Can I come in?" It looked as if he'd left his hat and coat downstairs with Kathleen. Mutely, Lydia stepped away from the doorway, and Henry followed her into her room.

"I hate to think that I've hurt you, Lydia. I wanted to explain—"

A brittle laugh from Lydia interrupted him. "God, Henry. D'you think it'd be difficult for me to find a man if I was desperate for one?"

Silence. Henry looked out of the frosty window.

"No," he said finally. "I know you understand that we could never be more than we already are to one another, but what I don't know is why you are so angry."

For a minute, Lydia contemplated this. Was she grieving—and hiding that grief even from herself—for the possibility of a life as Mrs. Shadwell? She tried to imagine it: herself and Henry, an ordinary couple, hand-clasped at a church altar; Henry taking her maidenhead on their wedding night; childbirth in a big bed with bleached white sheets; a clean, swaddled baby handed to her afterwards and received with a wan smile; the charming and demure hostess at dinner parties for Henry's fellow surgeons . . . Finally, with a sigh, she spoke.

"I'm not content, Henry, and I won't say that I don't care for you—more than I'd like to, 'specially now. But I don't think I know *how* to be a wife."

Henry nodded. "Then why were you so angry when you learned of my engagement?"

Softening, Lydia sat down on the bed, patting the sheets beside her.

"If there's anything of being Mrs. Shadwell that I'd want, it's a home of my own. But it wouldn't be my own, would it?"

Henry shook his head as he sat down next to her. "No. My home is mine, just as it will be when I am married and take Pearl to live with me."

"Pearl?" She'd never thought of Henry's intended having a name other than "Mrs. Shadwell." "Like the earrings you bought me for Christmas."

"I was in the jeweller's shop buying Pearl's betrothal ring when I found them. But I was thinking of you, Lydia. I care for you. It's time I married and had a family, and I cannot do that with you, but I don't want us to be separated. You are more to me than just a prostitute, or a model, or . . ." He tailed off, and Lydia knew that he was thinking of the night in the cemetery. "I do think of you as a friend, Lydia. You're impossible sometimes, but I hate to think that I've upset you." He sighed, raking his fingers through his hair, leaving it somewhat dishevelled. "Foolish of me, I suppose. I don't know why I expected it to work."

"Been working this long, hasn't it?" Hesitantly, she rested her hand beside Henry's on the bedsheets, their fingers brushing. "I reckon most of the men that come in here are married."

"It's not the same."

She flopped back on the bed and stared at the ceiling.

"P'raps not. I've never really known what to think of it, actually."

"You and I?"

"Yes. I used to think it was 'cause you do different things when we fuck than what I'm used to; but you're a man like any other, ain't you?"

"Oh, thank you." Henry smiled, and Lydia smiled back.

"You know what I mean."

"Yes, I do." Henry laid his palm flat on Lydia's tight-laced belly, and she lay quite still. As his fingers trailed down to lift the hem of her skirt, she forced herself to think of the mysterious Pearl, and Henry's future nuptials. The thought burned into her like a lit cigar driven into her flesh, but she accepted his caresses all the same. For a while, she had feared that she would never feel them again.

A torrent of ecstasy swirled around in the trails of his fingers. He rolled onto her, and Lydia, realizing that she had lain as still as a bride until that point, reached down to free him from his trousers and take him in her hand. His gaze on her face was curious, as though he could sense the distractions plaguing her, but his concerned expression was soon lost in an ecstatic smile. With the little room she had to move, she pushed up under him in tiny thrusts that sent a lascivious delight coursing up inside her.

· · ·

With a triumphant gasp, Henry rolled onto his back and lay beside her, his trousers unbuttoned.

"Then we're friends?" he asked finally. Looking across at Henry—earnest and exhausted—Lydia swallowed hard. Reaching across to him, she fussed with his hair and pushed it back from his face.

" 'Course we are."

Henry reached up, cupping Lydia's chin in his hand, then pulling her down and kissing her. With her lips pressed against his, Lydia chuckled.

"Let's clean you up, shall we?"

He left after she had cleaned him up for a second time (the first necessitating the second), paying both Lydia and Kathleen in full. Lydia slipped back upstairs as soon as she could, stashing her share of the money in the rag bundle. The thought of being Henry's kept mistress wasn't such a bad one. Perhaps.

Lydia and Mary were out walking in town the next day when they heard a yell.

"Oi, Mary!" Ellie Meakin, another local whore, was waving to them. She was accompanied by two friends. "I take it you've not heard, then," she said as they approached.

"I haven't the first clue what you're prattling about." There wasn't much love lost between Mary and Ellie, but they tolerated each other with glass-brittle smiles and barbs passed off as humour.

"About your Matty? Oh, he's been taken up, you know, for the coining. They arrested him in the Bull this morning—everyone's spoken of nothing else since. Lord, how did it not get to you before now?"

"He's what?" Mary's pink face had turned pale.

"A couple of bluebottles—they came in this morning and hauled him away. Apparently he'd passed some of his fakes to someone in town; we're all trying to work out who."

"You don't think it was someone in the Bull what turned him in, do you?" one of the other girls gasped. Mary looked dumbly at Lydia. They both knew well enough that Matty wasn't averse to paying for drinks in the Bull with his pewter money.

Ellie puffed out her cheeks, shaking her head.

"If they did, they certainly didn't say nothing to Alice; she looked as surprised as the rest of us. Anyway," she added, her voice sweet as a ratcatcher's bait, "listen to me going on, when I only meant to ask after you, Mary! You two were quite the sweethearts, weren't you?"

Mary said nothing, and Lydia took hold of her friend's wrist, glaring at Ellie as she tried to lead her away.

"You're quite right, Lydia—she shouldn't be standing around in the freezing cold out here when she's had such awful news," Ellie said. "All the bit fakers I've heard about recently got life."

Lydia looked helplessly at Mary as they walked away. It was true enough: the Lancaster Assizes was well known for being unforgiving. Enough people had been throttled on the end of the hangman's rope up there for the place to have earned the grim nickname of "Hanging Town" among the locals—they'd have no qualms about sending the likes of Matty away for a few decades. Mary shook off Lydia's grip and stalked wordlessly away.

A few feet up the road, Mary was already scrambling into the back of a cab. Yelling to the driver to wait, Lydia caught hold of the hem of her friend's skirt.

"Where are you going?"

Tears had begun to streak down Mary's face, but her voice was chillingly calm.

"To the jail, of course, where else? I have to see if it's true; I'm not trusting that Ellie Meakin."

Lydia stuck her hands into the pockets in her skirt, but both were empty, just as she had expected. Her money was tucked away safely under her bed at the introduction house. She leaned over to whisper in Mary's ear.

"Have you got the fare?"

Mary arched an eyebrow, her blue eyes hard and

glassy with tears. "I've no money on me, but I said he'd get something once we got there."

"He's taking you to the prison in exchange for a fuck?"

Mary looked levelly at her. "He thinks he is."

"Are you coming or not?" the driver shouted irritably from the front.

Lydia looked up at Mary, who sat resolutely still. Sighing, she vaulted up beside her friend, and the cab pulled away.

"Come on, Mary," she pleaded as they headed out of town, "we both know what Matty got up to: he was going to get in trouble sooner or later. It's not even as though he were careful."

Mary shook her head and picked at a loose thread on her shawl.

"I'm not surprised, and I know it won't do no good, but I'm still going to see him. D'you understand?"

Lydia thought of Henry, and the confusion he always seemed to cause her. She remembered Mary's girlish confession of love, and the back of her neck prickled.

"Yes. I understand."


The driver had scarcely slowed as he approached the massive red brick wall surrounding the prison when Lydia and Mary threw open the cab door and hopped out, leaving the door flapping and banging in the breeze as they ran away as fast as they could. They were gone before the driver had even realized what was happening, and hid around a corner until his infuriated bellowing stopped and they could creep out and approach the doors of the prison.

Lydia suspected that their pinned hems and painted faces had gone some way to persuading the warden to let Mary see Matty. Once inside, they followed the clank of the jailer's keys up the echoing metal steps and along the rows of cells. Mary kept her head down and ploughed resolutely forward, but Lydia could not stop herself gazing around as they climbed up past floor after floor of narrow cell doors. Inside, the prison was shaped like a vast cockfighting pit, with layers of cells lining each wall, and the staircases in the middle, leading up from the stone floor at the bottom. When Lydia looked up, the prison continued to stretch out above her, and she clutched at the banister, suddenly dizzy. Then the guard abruptly turned right, and they followed him towards Matty's cell.

"Right, that's as far as you go," the screw said, putting out a hand to stop Lydia. "Only one visitor at a time." Gesturing to a cell ahead, he told Mary to make it quick and slid the door hatch open to allow her to see in. At once Mary gasped, pressing her fingertips against her lips as she stared through the hatch at her sweetheart. Her legs still trembling from running away from the cabbie, Lydia leaned against the railings and glanced down at the cavernous drop below, where two guards were leading a handful of silent prisoners in from the yard and back to their cells. Outside Matty's cell, Mary was whispering, her fingers twisting through the holes she'd made in her shawl. Lydia couldn't hear what she was saying.

Matty's thin, grubby arm poked out through the hatch, reaching for Mary's cheek.

"Oi! Hands inside!" the screw shouted. The arm withdrew, and Mary spoke some more. The jailer turned to face Lydia, and she stared blankly past him at her friend. Whatever Matty's reply, it brought tears to Mary's eyes. She swept her fingers against her cheeks, before stepping forward and laying her palms against the solid door. Instantly, the jailer was at her side.

"Right, you've had your time. C'mon, I've got work to do."

"So what did he say?" Lydia asked once they were outside. Mary's eyes were damp and pink-rimmed. She sighed.

"The idiot paid a bloke selling watches with one of his fake coins, and it turns out he chose the wrong man.

The police have been wanting to catch him out for months. They've terrier-cropped his hair already." Her voice quavered, and she reached for the gold locket hung around her neck and snapped it open. It was still empty inside. "I never did remember to ask him for a lock, and now he's all but bald. He looks a right mess."

"So what now?"

"They'll take him up to Lancaster for the Lent Assizes but they'll keep him in Preston for now, which is probably best. The cells at Lancaster are supposed to be even worse." She sighed heavily.

Mary fell silent, eventually nodding.

"I'm going to go up to Lancaster in March. I can't bear the thought of it, but I have to go. If they . . ." Lydia nodded, gripping her friend's wrist in her cold fingers. "If they put him away for good, then I should be there. I want to be there for him when he's up in court. I want him to be able to see a friendly face when . . . when they make their decision. I told him he's to look at me when that happens—me and no one else."

"Aye, if you think that's best," Lydia replied gently. "You know they're going to send him down, though. You said yourself they've wanted to catch him for ages."

Mary heaved a huge, shuddering sigh.

## 15

To a stranger visiting Kathleen Tanner's introduction house, the days immediately following Matty's arrest would have seemed normal. Indeed, Mary and Lydia went about their work more fervently than ever, with Lydia even attempting to draw some enjoyment from the better-looking men who passed through her room. Invariably, though, she knew she would not have fucked them for free.

Meanwhile, Mary's demeanour swung between a ferocity it had never previously known, sending howls of real pain through the house, and an apathetic listlessness that left her customers dissatisfied.

One quiet afternoon, when the baker's lad had delivered

her newspaper, Lydia slipped out, with the pretext of
picking up the soap that Connie had forgotten to buy.
Once she had bought the soap, she whipped the newspaper out from under her arm and flicked to the property advertisements. Annabel had not deigned to reply
to her letter, but she could still do something about her
living arrangements. Rooms on Deepdale Road and
around Winckley Square were quickly discounted—only
servicing a rich man could provide that kind of place.
Running the tip of her finger along the lines of heavy
black print, she searched and searched until, with a hot
little flutter in her chest, she found one.

> **Accommodation available for rent—**
> **comfortable property on Fishergate.**
> **Apply to Mrs. Ruth Bell . . .**

The clock on the tower atop the Baptist church was
striking two o'clock. Checking the address before
clamping the paper underneath her arm, Lydia set off as
fast as she could down towards Fishergate.

It was only when she presented herself on the doorstep
of the advertised house that she remembered her appearance. Her bodice was cut too low for any decent young

woman, and she had forgotten to remove her paint. Peering at her reflection in the front window—the room inside was mercifully empty—she fished a handkerchief out of the top of her dress, spat on it, and scrubbed at the black around her eyes and the red on her lips. From inside came the sound of a door closing and footfall on floorboards. Lydia swore under her breath. Hoping she had removed most of the paint (the reflection in the window was not a good one), she yanked the crown brooch from her skirts and kicked the hem down to hide her petticoats. For the first time in memory, she felt shy. As the door opened, she pulled her shawl tightly around herself, hiding the offending neckline.

"Yes?" The woman looked like an older Kathleen, neither welcoming nor forbidding. A short, stooped figure with sharp blue eyes and hair that was fading from brown to grey, she was dressed well, in a black mourning frock of thick, warm-looking cloth, but something in her steady gaze told Lydia that this was not a woman who had been born to such comforts.

Lydia cleared her throat and made her voice sound as innocent as possible.

"Mrs. Bell?"

"Aye, that's me. What are you wanting, then?" The landlady's voice confirmed Lydia's suspicions, and for a moment her nerve weakened. Would Mrs. Bell see her for what she really was?

"I—I'm here about the advertisement, in the news-paper. I'm looking for accommodation."

Mrs. Bell did not look surprised, and Lydia doubted she was the first lone girl the landlady had dealt with.

"I see. Well, you'd best come in then, Miss . . . ?"

"Ketch. Lydia Ketch." As soon as she said it, she felt sick—should she have given another name?

But Mrs. Bell was already ushering her in through the front door. It was painted a dark green, and a brass horseshoe was nailed above the knocker. "Miss Ketch. Come in, I'll show you the room."

In the hallway, a fat ginger cat lazed at the foot of the stairs. Lydia's legs were already trembling. Carefully lift-ing her skirts she stepped over the cat—one foot and then the other—and onto the staircase.

"That's Jonah," Mrs. Bell said.

"Who?" For a moment Lydia wondered if Mrs. Bell had a male boarder, or perhaps several.

"The cat."

"Oh!" Relieved, she gave what she hoped was a care-free, innocent smile.

"He don't trouble any of the boarders—just make sure you don't leave any food or milk out in the kitchen unless you want it stolen, and watch your footing when you're walking around outside your room. He keeps the place free of rats and mice, though, and he does it at no extra charge to you." The landlady winked and Lydia laughed nervously.

"They're just single rooms, I'm afraid."

"Oh, that's no bother at all," Lydia said. Her words felt like they were coming too quickly.

"We do have a bathroom you can use, with hot water, too. Here we are." She produced a key from her apron pocket and turned it in the lock of a cream-painted door.

"Here we are," Mrs. Bell said again. She stepped back, allowing Lydia to walk into the room. It was small—smaller than her quarters at Kathleen's, and smaller than she'd been expecting. Still, it was clean, and the leaded window looking out onto the street below gave it a good light. And it would be hers.

Looking around, Lydia thought she could probably squeeze a small writing desk and stool in, if she ever got around to buying them. She walked over to a tall cupboard that stood against a wall papered with fading roses and vines. The hinges squeaked a little as she opened the door.

"It's a wardrobe," Mrs. Bell said. "Not a large one, but it'll do you."

"For clothes, you mean?"

" 'Course. You never had one before?"

"I'm used to keeping my clothes in my trunks. There weren't any wardrobes at . . ." *Think of something, girl!* ". . . At school. I've been away at school."

"I see." Mrs. Bell tutted and bent to slap a tattered cobweb off the foot of the bed. "So what brings you back to Preston then? You sound like a local girl."

"I came back after the death of my father." Lydia's mind raced. "I'm the only surviving Ketch, so I inherited his business." An idea came to her. "He was a printer. I've had to take up the reins."

Mrs. Bell didn't seem surprised. "This place were my husband's. I've had to give up with the rent books—can't fathom 'em for the life of me. But I always know who's got rent owing," she added.

Lydia smiled. "You needn't worry about me, Mrs. Bell. Speaking of rent . . ."

"Four shillings a week. If you do move in, I'll be wanting two weeks in advance."

"I can give you a month." Lydia had no idea whether four shillings was reasonable for rented accommodation, but she forced down a chuckle as she realized that one week at Mrs. Bell's cost the same as one of Kathleen's rooms did for the duration of a shag.

"That'd be grand," said the landlady. "D'you want to pay now? You can move straight in."

Lydia rummaged in her pocket for her purse. Anticipating this, she had brought a little of her savings along with her, and she pressed the coins into Mrs. Bell's weathered palm, silently counting them as she went. The old woman checked the amount and fingered the coins for signs of forgery before stuffing them into her apron pocket.

"I'll bring my things in a few days," Lydia promised.

"I'll see you then."

. . .

Back at the introduction house, Lydia dug around in her pocket and handed the cake of soap to Kathleen.

"Took you long enough," said the abbess.

"I wanted to get a paper, too," she replied. "For Mary. She don't want to miss Matty's trial."

Kathleen grunted. "Have they announced the next Assizes, then?" The news of the coiner's arrest had spread like cholera through Preston's gutters, and the abbess had soon appreciated the connection to Mary's melancholia. Her anger, though ferocious, had quickly subsided: after all, Matty would no longer be sniffing around Mary.

Lydia was with a man when Henry showed up late that night. She heard the scuffle downstairs and Kathleen yelling after someone. Lydia's client buttoned his flap and opened her door to leave, only to have Henry barrel into him.

"Good God, man—can't you wait your turn?"

"This is urgent." Henry ushered him out onto the landing, shutting the door behind him. Lydia laughed and scooped a handful of water out of her basin.

"I should keep you on hand to throw 'em all out," she said after she'd spat the water back into the bowl. "It'd save me a lot of time." A warm glow hummed in her stomach, and a girlish smile spread across her face. "Then again, I shan't be here much longer. I went to see a land-lady about a room today, and—"

"Lydia . . ." The tone of Henry's voice quenched the warmth inside her, and her voice dwindled to a whisper.

"What? What is it?"

"I just went over to the hospital to collect some specimens . . . One of them was from the locked ward, Lydia. The venereal cases."

She knew now what he was going to say, but she had to hear it, regardless. "Henry?"

"It's Daisy. She died three days ago. I'm sorry, Lydia."

"You said the clap wouldn't kill her!"

Henry toyed with the white cuffs of his shirt, but his eyes were steady on Lydia's. "It didn't. The locked wards hardly represent the best in medical care. The patients are kept cramped together, allowing disease to spread, and that's to say nothing of the surgeons." He looked pointedly at Lydia. "And Daisy was already weakened by her existing infection. I'm certain that's why she suc-cumbed so quickly."

Lydia sat down heavily on the edge of the bed. Another friend dead, and Lydia had not been able to save her. There were still nights when she woke in the small hours after dreaming of Jimmy, when she would wrap herself tightly in her blankets and tell herself over and over again that she'd been little more than a babby when he died, that she wasn't to know that he'd eat the bacon he found out in the yard. But she wasn't a babby any more, and still her friends were dying around her. Not five minutes ago, she'd been optimistic about the future, but now . . .

"So where is she now?" she said eventually.

"She's at my rooms."

In her mind's eye, Lydia saw the dingy, yellowing walls of the dissection room. "Henry, you're not thinking of . . . ?"

He began to speak but a gasp from Lydia silenced him. She screwed up her eyes as though doing so would block out the pictures she saw of her friend filleted and boned like a fish on a market stall. Instantly, Henry was beside her on the bed, pulling her into his arms. She pressed her cheek against his chest, and listened to the resonant beat of his heart.

"No, I'm not. Daisy was your friend, I know that." Henry smoothed Lydia's hair away from her face, running his fingers along her cheeks as if to wipe away the tears she felt unable to cry. "And now that my lessons with my students are complete, I shall be reducing the numbers of bodies I use quite dramatically."

Lydia gulped. "Really?"

"Yes. Well, I am a qualified surgeon; there is little I need to practise now. I may perform an occasional dissection, but Daisy will not be one of them."

Kathleen and Mary were waiting at the foot of the stairs as they descended.

"Mr. Shadwell," Kathleen said tersely, "I know you have been a good customer, but let me assure you that does not give you licence to push me out of the way, in my own house, when I tell you that Lydia is occupied."

"Mrs. Tanner, I assure *you*—"

"He's had word of Daisy," Lydia said, before they came to blows. She looked to Henry to deliver the news.

"You see, Mrs. Tanner, I have an understanding with certain people regarding the . . . procuring of specimens . . ."

Lydia cringed.

"So you're a bloody sawbones. What's this got to do with Daisy?"

"Mrs. Tanner, Mary . . . I collect the dead from the locked wards and the charity hospitals. And so I can tell you that your girl is deceased. She picked up an infection while in hospital, it seems. I'm sorry."

Suddenly Mary flew at Henry, fingers hooked into claws. Lydia stepped between them and caught her wrists. Mary screamed incoherent abuse at Henry, cursing Lydia for a traitor. "I know you're fucking him, Lydia, but how dare you stand there and simper like a slut over the man who wants to carve up our friend?" she shrieked. "Our friend, Lydia!"

Lydia released one of Mary's hands just long enough to slap her friend hard across the face.

"He's not going to carve her up, you stupid cow!" she spat back. Mary's struggling slowed, and Lydia let her go. "He came to tell us so we can arrange a decent burial for her, and move her back here until the undertaker collects her." Her gaze alighted on Kathleen, whose eyes were flicking guiltily towards the open parlour door. "We can lay her out in her old room instead of the parlour, can't we? No one'd know then, and we can bury her properly."

Mary leaned back against the wall, sinking down onto her haunches, and Kathleen nodded slowly.

"I've got a bit of money put away. I'll see her right."

# 16

Daisy was buried in the cemetery later that week. Lydia, Mary, Kathleen and several of the regulars from the Bull stood around her graveside, dressed in their most sober clothes, as the vicar commended Daisy's body to the soil and her soul to God's mercy. A crow perched on top of a nearby monument, its throaty caw shattering the silence as Mary took the first handful of soil to cast into the grave. An empty space had opened up inside Lydia, and it seemed to be expanding with each passing minute.

*What if God ain't being merciful to Daisy now?* Lydia wondered silently. *Or if He can't allow any whores into Heaven? Is selling your body like having it chopped up, and you're never whole again?*

The bowl of earth had been passed around the group of mourners now, and only a little was left in the bottom for Kathleen. She took it, arching an eyebrow in a silent challenge to the vicar as he stared disapprovingly at her, and scattered it into the grave with the rest. The soft soil pattered lightly on the smooth wooden lid of Daisy's coffin, and Mary buried her tear-stained face in Lydia's shoulder. Lydia murmured soothingly, but inside she felt as though her stomach had been slit open. There was so much she had wanted to say to Daisy, and it scarcely seemed possible that she would never have a chance to do so.

Kathleen closed the house to visitors that night, and Lydia and Mary went for a drink in the Bull, to wish Daisy well on her journey. Alice was tending the bar when they went in, and she wouldn't take their money for their first brandies of the evening.

"Bloody criminal is what it is," she muttered as she sloshed the liquor out into their glasses. "Whatever Daisy had done in her time, locking her up in that place to catch her death was ten times worse—and her not yet twenty! You two want to be careful, you know. You don't want to follow her, do you?"

Mary smiled ironically. "Never thought of that, had we, Lydia?"

They stayed in the taproom until closing time, huddled

together in the corner by the fire where Daisy had been sitting the day she was arrested, tipping measure after measure of brandy down their throats in a bid to swallow its warmth and dull the awful emptiness inside. They stayed that way for hours, only getting up in turn to visit the bar and fetch more brandy, until the landlord came round after last orders to usher everyone out. The girls stumbled out onto the frozen footpath, tripping over their trailing skirts and clinging to one another in an attempt to keep themselves from falling, and, weaving from one side of the path to the other, turned to head back to Kathleen's.

At first, when Lydia caught sight of the unkempt man approaching them, as they made their way past St. John's, she paid him no mind. Indeed, her vision was so clouded in her haze of brandy she had barely seen him at all, but as he stormed towards them, she slowly became aware that she had seen him before: the scaldrum dodger who'd made his sores from blood and soap. He was shouting incoherently, and Lydia realized that he'd had a few drinks himself that evening, probably bought with money begged from strangers.

"Well, if it ain't the two little ladies," he sneered, attempting to shove his hand into his jacket pocket and missing altogether. "I see you've got money to spare to have a drink yourselves, then."

Mary clutched at Lydia's arm. "Let's just go, Lydia."

"Yes, run away!" the man bellowed as they stepped

around him and hurried away as fast as their drunken pace would allow them. His voice was still close behind; he was following them. "Run back and hide in your bloody whorehouse, under the sheets paid for by half the men of Preston, you filthy slags. There's none of that easy money for men like me, is there?" A heavy hand landed on Mary's shoulder, and she shrieked as the beggar hauled her around to face him, venom in his eyes.

"The likes of you don't know what hardship is." He shoved Mary to the ground, and she landed on her backside in the gutter with the cigar ends and the horseshit. Incensed, Lydia turned on the man and slapped him across the face, her long nails leaving claw-marks on his cheek.

"We don't know what hardship is? Don't know what it is? I could tell you more tales of misery in a week than most folk know in a lifetime, you pathetic old shiteface!" She got no further before he punched her in the face, bloodying her nose and sending her reeling backwards. She heard Mary's scream, but it sounded muffled compared with the pounding of her own heart. The beggar lurched for her again, and Lydia pushed him hard, sending him stumbling drunkenly onto his knees in front of her. As she turned away a sickening pain shot through her thigh and she groaned. Her eyes darted down, and there she saw it: the gleaming steel blade of a knife stabbed into her thigh through her skirts. Mary screamed again, and the scaldrum dodger's eyes widened in alarm.

Before Lydia could move, he grabbed the handle of the knife and yanked the blade from her flesh, running away as fast as his skinny legs would carry him.

Lydia sagged against the low wall surrounding the parish church. The world seemed to be spinning giddily around her, and she could feel the hot blood slipping down her thigh. Mary screamed and screamed for help, soft hands patting Lydia's pale cheeks as her head lolled sleepily and she disappeared down a cold pit of pink and yellow stars.

When she stirred her eyes felt as though sand had been sprinkled under the lids. Squinting, she slowly became accustomed to the flickering light and warmth of a nearby fire. Feeling a sudden pain in her thigh, she looked down to see Henry patting the wound clean with a wet cloth. He smiled nervously.

"There you are. I thought you might wake soon."

She turned her stiff neck and looked around, recognizing Kathleen's parlour. They must have asked Connie to relight the fire, and fetch the bowl of clean water that rested at Henry's feet. Lydia lay stretched out on the couch, an old sheet tucked under her bloodstained leg to protect the embroidery.

"How did I get here?"

"Kathleen sent for me. She's upstairs with Mary, getting your bed ready for you."

Lydia's stomach flipped at the thought of Kathleen being in her room, and she hoped she'd hidden all her writing stuff well before she'd left for the Bull.

"Did they catch him?"

"Your attacker? No, I'm afraid not. Mary says he ran away, and her first concern was getting you to safety." Henry paused for a moment, scrutinizing her face before returning his attentions to the gently seeping hole in her thigh. A leather belt had been pulled tight around her upper leg to stem the bleeding, and beside his fingers, what looked like a plump black slug was sucking greedily at the edge of the wound. Instinctively, Lydia jumped and flicked at it with the tip of a fingernail, but the creature held tightly to her leg. With his left hand, Henry caught hold of her wrist before she could attack again.

"What the hell—" Lydia protested.

"It's just a leech." Still holding onto her wrist, Henry shook her pale hand with each word he spoke, as if to drive his point home further. "The wound is congested; it needs to be drained if it is to heal. It won't be on for much longer, and then I'll get the wound safely sutured and dressed."

Lydia grimaced, but did not protest further. Instead she gazed at her punctured thigh: a strange glimpse of the inside of her own body, so familiar and yet so unrecognizable. She eyed the leech with revulsion: a slick, shiny sliver of black against her flesh.

"I think we're almost there," Henry murmured, half to himself, before turning and looking into Lydia's eyes.

"You've been lucky," he was saying. "The blade didn't rupture any major veins or cause damage to the bone. There's just one small piece of tissue here that will not heal." He gestured with the bloodstained swab at a particularly ragged patch of flesh. "It will need to be cut away before I can suture the wound." Turning in his seat, he reached into his bag and fished out a brown glass bottle with a faded label. "I have some chloroform—"

"No!" The violence of Lydia's reaction startled Henry, and he looked at her with an expression of confusion.

"I can't stand the smell of the stuff," she explained, lowering her voice lest Kathleen hear the commotion upstairs.

"Oh, have you needed anaesthesia in the past?"

She shook her head. "I've never been put to sleep, if that's what you mean, but Daisy . . . Daisy was a few times. Kathleen had a little bottle that she kept aside for when we had a chap who liked his girls sick and wasting—it were easier for her to pass as consumptive."

Lydia's eyes welled up with tears that escaped and trickled down her cheeks before she had time to stop them. Without asking what the matter was, Henry pulled her close to him, shattering what remained of her resistance and causing her to sob helplessly.

"Fucking marvellous," she gasped through her tears.

"I'm surprised that it's taken this long."

"I'm not crying over my leg."

"I know." Henry's shirtfront was soaked now, and Lydia palmed away the tears left on her face.

"Come on then," she said, "let's get this over with."

"Without the chloroform? It will hurt, you know."

Lydia nodded decisively. "Then it'll just have to hurt, won't it?"

Henry plucked the swollen leech from her leg with a pair of tweezers and returned it to a jar of greenish water. Moving down to her injured leg, he loosened the belt around her thigh, adjusting the tourniquet's pressure until he was satisfied. Then he reached for his tray of tools and lifted out a tiny pair of tweezers and a small, sharp knife. The sound of metal on metal made Lydia cringe, but she couldn't stop herself lifting her head to watch. She winced as Henry took hold of the torn piece of flesh in the fine tips of the tweezers. Even as he moved the blade closer, she didn't look away. Her breathing was coming fast and shallow, hissing through her nose and around the cloth in her mouth. As he swept the ruined tissue from her leg with a single stroke of the blade, she stifled a scream.

Henry examined the hole. "Now I need to suture the wound," he said.

Lydia wasn't sure which was worse—the sharp prick of the needle or the trailing of the catgut through the tiny holes in her flesh. She forced herself to lie still.

After both sides of the hole in her thigh had been sewn shut and Kathleen and Mary had come downstairs to tell her that her room was ready, Henry lifted Lydia in his arms and carried her up to her bed. As they crossed the parlour threshold, she shot a wry look at him. Once they were alone in her room, she lay on the bed, propped up on the pillows and sipping at the glass of brandy Henry had sent Connie to fetch.

"It were brandy that got me into this mess," Lydia grumbled.

"This is different, it's medicinal. You make a good patient," Henry said, smiling. "You're extremely stoical."

"Eh?"

"You tolerate unpleasant things very well."

"Oh. Well, I've had a lot of practice." Lydia wriggled on the pillows, making herself more comfortable. The wound was sticking to the sheets and hurt like hell, but she hadn't the strength to hold it off the mattress. The brandy was starting to make her head spin.

"I dropped in on John Fletcher the other day," Henry said, his voice warm and encouraging. "You met him when he came to my workshop to collect some pictures?"

Lydia nodded. "Aye, I remember. Seems a lifetime ago, though."

Henry patted her hand reassuringly. "He's selling *The White Flowers Reader* in his shop, you know," he said quietly. "He says it's doing nicely: you did well to let it be known that it was written by a woman. That's an appealing idea for many men."

A weak smile tugged at the corners of Lydia's mouth.

"It's looking hopeful, Lydia. You wanted to earn your living selling your paper, and it seems as though you'll be able to do so. And you have your new home waiting for you—why delay any longer?"

"I'll tell Kathleen tomorrow," she whispered.

"Wonderful. I hope I'll still be a welcome visitor, though, when you move out into accommodation of your own." Henry winked.

"I thought you were going to be happily wed, mister? Hammered for life and all that?"

"I'll be wed, all right, and Pearl seems a pleasant enough girl. I'm sure she'll make an excellent wife."

Lydia nodded, tipping the brandy glass to her lips

again. "And what makes an excellent wife ain't what you're always after, is it?"

"Hardly."

A silence ensued, and Henry topped up Lydia's glass and gulped brandy from the bottle himself. Lydia licked her dry lips.

"What's she like?"

"Pearl?"

"No, Princess Beatrice. 'Course I meant Pearl."

"Are you sure you want to ask me that?"

"Yes—I'm not the excellent wife type, remember? I don't ask questions just to be polite, I ask 'cause I want to know the answers."

Henry exhaled thoughtfully. "She's a nice girl. Quiet, seems to be gentle and caring. She's the daughter of a tobacco merchant I met at a dinner party." He stole a glance at Lydia before continuing. "Poor thing goes quite pale whenever I visit, although she assures me she does want the wedding to go ahead. I think it's just nerves—at least, I hope it is. She's a sweet girl, I don't want to frighten the creature to death."

Lydia tried to imagine what it would be like to be afraid of bedding down with a man. She wondered if, given a different life, she herself would have swooned at the thought.

"So," she said, taking a gulp of brandy and holding it in her mouth to savour the warming sensation, "when's the happy day?"

"Thursday. Thursday morning."

Lydia counted on her fingers. "So that's one . . . two . . . three days away." She shook her head in amazement, and Henry soon followed suit.

"I know." He hesitated. "Lydia, you never answered my question. Will you let me visit you once you're set up in your new home?"

"Aye. You know I will."

Henry leaned over and kissed the corner of her mouth.

"So where are these new lodgings of yours, then?"

## 17

When Lydia awoke the following morning, the fire was still flickering away in the hearth and there was a jug of water at her bedside. Grimacing, she shifted under the covers. Mary brought her breakfast in bed, and Lydia propped herself up on the pillows. It was kippers and scrambled egg, and Mary had cut the fish into little morsels for Lydia to skewer with her fork. She smiled, half amused and half touched, and silently thanked God that Kathleen hadn't sent up any of her underdone bacon.

"I'll bring you some broth later on, too," Mary was saying. "Then you can stay in bed."

Lydia shook her head as she took her friend's hand. "I'll get up. There's things I need to do."

Mary's blue eyes were wide. "What on God's earth is so important you want to be doing it now?"

Lydia glanced across at the closed door of her bedroom and lowered her voice. "I've rented a room down Fishergate. I paid a month's rent in advance, and all I have to do is take my things and move in. I want to do it today, before anything else can happen to me. Next time it could be a knife in my throat or my ribs, and I don't want to wait and see which. I'll take my things over first then come back and face Kathleen."

"You're leaving?" Mary had turned pale, and Lydia's stomach churned.

"I'm not leaving Preston altogether. I'll be down by the station, that's all: number six. The house has a green door with a horseshoe nailed to it." She grinned ruefully. "Thought it might bring me luck."

Mary smiled half-heartedly in reply, and Lydia squeezed her cold fingers in her own.

"How're you going to pay your way?"

At first, Mary didn't believe her when she told her about her arrangement with Stan the Frenchman, but eventually Lydia was able to persuade her that—she hoped—she wouldn't starve alone in her new lodgings. She had suggested that Mary could go with her when she moved, but her friend had smiled weakly and changed the subject.

Matty's arrest seemed to have dulled Mary's urge to leave Kathleen's.

There was no frost that morning, and she was able to sweet-talk Kathleen into letting her go out for a fresh loaf of bread. Henry had told the abbess that a little exercise and fresh air would aid her recovery; indeed, he had left a walking stick for her to use if she needed it. Lydia worried that she did not have much time. How long would it be before Kathleen came to realize what she was planning?

"Good to see you looking so much better, Lydia," the abbess said as she left, her smile unconvincing. "P'raps you'll be up to seeing a few fellows this afternoon, after all."

Lydia nodded. Even now, she had no idea how she would break the news to the abbess that she would never see another fellow again unless she chose to.

Outside, a string dangled just within reach from the sill of her bedroom window. She'd bundled her money, her pens and ink and paper, into a cloth bag along with her clothes and her copies of *The White Flowers Reader*, and set it out on the windowsill before leaving. Stretching up on her toes, her face twisted in pain, Lydia caught the end of the string between two fingers and tugged it, pulling down the bag. She cringed as it passed the parlour window, her stomach churning. Then she drew a deep breath and threw her bag over her shoulder, hurrying off as fast as her wounded leg would allow towards the bustle of Fishergate. Through the teeth-gritting pain, she felt a smile come to her lips.

Moving in was the easy part. Although she had exclaimed over Lydia's limp and helped her upstairs with her bag, Mrs. Bell did not linger in Lydia's room. As the landlady shuffled off downstairs, talking loudly to Jonah about a kipper, Lydia allowed herself to look around. She was home. Even without speaking it aloud, the word sounded strange in her head. *Home.* The very *idea* felt strange. *Home.* She had no bedding (it had seemed unwise to take a set from Kathleen), but she could make do with her cloaks as blankets for the time being. She felt like she had all the time in the world.

On her way back, she dropped in on Stan the Frenchman before he closed up his shop for the evening. He wasn't busy, having just delivered some more stock to John Fletcher downstairs.

"So is it really true, then?" Lydia said. "Is my paper doing well?"

"So far," Stoker said, offering Lydia a stool. She sat down gingerly, wincing at the tugging in her stitches. "There's been about twenty-five copies sold; I'll give you your money before you leave. Don't look as if you've been doing so well, though. What's to do?"

Lydia shook her head dismissively. "Picked a fight with the wrong bloke, that's all. So, can I bring you some more to print up?"

"You can if you like. It's your paper, ain't it?"

Stan offered to walk back up to Fishergate with her. As they hiked up the gentle slope of Glovers Court, the way he kept glancing at her limping gait put Lydia on her guard, and she found herself wondering if she would ever be able to undo the suspicious nature she had acquired in her short life. When she stepped on an uneven cobblestone and her ankle threatened to give out, she instinctively reached out to the nearest wall to right herself instead of clutching the printer's arm, and the rough brickwork grazed the soft white heel of her palm.

As they reached Fishergate, a chiming of church bells announced that it was four o'clock. Stan swore.

"I'll go back and lock up now, I reckon. Come by again when you've got your next issue."

Lydia nodded, and Stan turned to head back to his shop. She stepped out onto Fishergate, stopping when she recognized the girl standing at the opposite side of the road.

. . .

Annabel was thinner still, and wore a dark brown dress that was too loose about the bodice. But Lydia would have recognized her face—eyes wide, lips slightly parted, like a startled child—anywhere. Wincing at the pain in her leg, she hurried towards her sister as quickly as she could, but stopped when she stepped away from her.

"Annie?"

Annabel didn't reply, but buried her chin in her shawl and strode away without looking back. Her steps hastened, and her shoulders were hunched, allowing her to draw her shawl around her face. Then she slipped into a crowd and Lydia lost sight of her.

Trying to make sense of what had just happened, she felt anger rising in her chest. In that moment, she hated them all: Annie for acting as if she'd never so much as seen an introduction house, Kathleen for her coldness, Mary for her short temper, Henry for . . . for what, exactly? And then there was Lydia herself, for caring enough about any of it to hate them at all.

With rage boiling in her belly, she set off back to the introduction house, hoping that her sour mood would last a day or so longer. Then she'd be able to walk away from Kathleen's without feeling the slightest ounce of guilt.

# 18

But when she arrived, Mary was waiting for her in the hallway. As soon as Lydia set foot in the house, her friend flapped her arms and tried to bundle her back outside, shushing her frantically when Lydia tried to ask what the hell was going on.

"Kathleen!" Mary hissed. "She's turned your room upside down while you've been gone. She—"

"*She knows what you're up to, missy!*" The girls whirled around to see the abbess standing imperiously at the top of the stairs. Her expression icy, Kathleen strode down to meet them.

"All that's left is your sodding sheets!" Elbowing

Mary out of the way, she took hold of Lydia's shawl and hauled her through the door.

"Just what do you think you're doing? Running off to be his kept piece, aren't you? That bloody surgeon of yours—I wish to God he'd never set foot in this place."

"We met in the Bull!" Lydia hissed.

Kathleen belted her around the back of the head, and she clung to the wall to stop herself falling. Shaking her head, she started to speak.

"I'm not leaving to be *his* mistress, or anyone else's. I'm going to pay my own way—I'm sick of the trade!"

Kathleen laughed. "You are, are you? And just how d'you think you're going to earn a living?"

"You did, didn't you? And before you hit me again, I'm not setting up a house of my own; I won't be taking any of your sodding customers. I was going to tell you, Kathleen . . . I wasn't just going to run off."

The abbess scoffed. "Good of you, I'm sure. You'd never have stood a chance without me, back when you first showed up on my doorstep like a couple of stray cats. Just how d'you think you'd have fed yourself and Annabel if I hadn't taken you in?"

"And I suppose you took me and Annie in out of the goodness of your heart?" She calmed slightly before continuing. "Kathleen, I am grateful you did. But I won't stay out of loyalty." She sighed and shifted her weight from one hip to the other. Her leg was hurting badly now.

Glaring, Kathleen threw open the front door and pushed Lydia out. "Shove it up your arse. I don't need you and I never have. Hobble back to whatever fleapit you've managed to find. I'll give Connie your room if I have to—at least she don't limp like an old woman and have a load of ideas above her station. You can go back to the gutter for all I care!"

Mary reached out to Lydia, but Kathleen slammed the door closed between them.

As she sat in her room at Mrs. Bell's, it was hard for her to stay angry. Her room was small, but as long as she kept up her rent, it was hers. And Kathleen hadn't been so bad, not really. Not that Lydia had the slightest intention of going back to her, but without Kathleen, she and Annie might well have followed their mother to the grave a year ago. And for all their squabbles, there was something Lydia could understand about Kathleen: she had that strange emptiness that seemed to accompany so many of those who had been in the trade: a ghostly stillness that haunted a girl's eyes. Lydia had seen it in her own reflection a couple of times as she sat in front of her mirror to brush her hair before bed, and now she wondered if it would be there for ever. She pulled a shawl about her shoulders and lay down on the bare mattress. Her leg ached, and her eyelids felt heavy.

She dozed for a while, waking only when a knock at the door jolted her back into consciousness. Briefly, she thought she was still at Kathleen's, but as she blinked the tiny room into view, she was startled a second time by a pair of inscrutable yellow-green eyes watching her from the small table at her bedside.

"Who is it?" she called out. Jonah yawned exuberantly, baring his dagger-like teeth and stretching his furry orange body before jumping down onto the floorboards with a soft thud and weaving his way out through the little gap where she'd left the door ajar.

"You should be more careful." Henry's head poked around the gap as Jonah's tail disappeared the other way. "Anyone could let themselves in." He looked at Lydia, and she nodded.

"How did you get her downstairs to let you in?"

Henry pointed to Lydia's leg. "I told her the truth. That you were wounded and that I was a surgeon and had come to check on you."

Lydia grinned. "Well, what d'you think of my new place, then?"

Henry nodded. "It's a lot like the room I had when I first moved to Preston. My room overlooked the station."

For a moment they looked at each other in silence, Lydia smoothing the bare mattress with the back of her hand.

"I assume you went to Kathleen's."

Henry smiled ruefully. "Yes. Most gentleman visitors never see the extent of her temper, do they?"

Lydia cackled. "She still thinks I've run off with you. My leg's doing all right, anyway." She flipped back her skirts and pulled the bandage aside, grimacing at the red-purple bruising around the stitches. "Went out on it this morning, and it were fine."

Henry leaned over to study the wound. "Yes, it looks fine. The stitches will be ready to come out in a week or two. What in God's name were you doing out, anyway?"

"Went to see Stan the Frenchman, if you must know." Her lips twitched upwards into a smile. "He's sold nearly every copy of my paper, and now he wants another." She looked up at Henry, mischief glittering in her eyes. "I'll need more stories to tell."

Henry laid a hand on the back of her head, his fingers twisting into the thick mass of her hair. "That's wonderful news. I shall have to pay Stan a visit and purchase a copy myself before supplies run out." The tip of his forefinger brushed the back of Lydia's neck, sending a shiver through her.

"As a matter of fact," Henry added, trailing his finger around her throat, "I have a spare typewriter back at my workshop. I'll bring it round, but you have to promise that you'll spend tomorrow in bed. You can type up your next paper before you deliver it to Stan." He smiled wryly. "Save the poor old chap having to read your scrawl."

Lydia poked her tongue out at him, and Henry reciprocated in kind before continuing.

"But no more carrying on all over town. You're to rest, d'you hear me?"

"Thank you, Mr. Shadwell." Lydia grinned mischievously. Lifting her wounded leg carefully, she slid back on the narrow bed, leaving just enough room for Henry to join her.

"I can see," he murmured, in between kisses, "that you don't understand the first thing about rest."

"Come and show me, then," she purred. "Quiet, though. And mind me leg."

After he'd dressed, Henry left to tend to a genuine patient, and Lydia walked across the room to close her door. As she laid a warm hand on the doorknob, the sound of voices drifted up from the hallway below, and unable to resist, she leaned closer and listened.

"She'll be fine, Mrs. Bell," Henry was saying. "It's a nasty injury, but Miss Ketch is young and strong. I have no doubt that she'll heal nicely."

Mrs. Bell hummed an agreement. "Is there owt I can do to help?"

"I don't think so, Mrs. Bell. As long as she gets plenty of rest and takes care when she does go out, I'm sure she'll be fine." His voice was louder and clearer now; for her benefit, Lydia suspected. "And make sure you pester her if she doesn't take the time to rest. I can't be here every minute to persuade her to get back into bed."

Shaking her head in silent amusement, Lydia went to the window to wave to him as he headed back into town. In the street, carts and carriages and the occasional omnibus rattled over the cobbles, and people with shopping baskets mingled with the street-sellers, either pushing through the crowds to get to the barrows and the girls with trays around their necks, or assiduously avoiding them. For a moment, Lydia wished she could see over to the station. She remembered the long afternoons she had spent there with her tray of boot and corset laces. With a grin, she turned away from the window and the bustle in the street below, and stretched out on her bed.

Henry was as good as his word, delivering the typewriter early the following morning. Again his knocking at her door woke Lydia from a deep sleep, and they sat on the narrow bed, Lydia still slouching in her camisole and under-petticoat, while he showed her how to feed a sheet of paper into the heavy, ugly contraption, and how to start typing out her words.

"I can't stay too long," he warned. "I have . . . things to attend to."

"For your wedding, you mean?" Lydia had come to realize that this was one of the few subjects that made Henry uncomfortable, and now, whenever he hesitated, she assumed that thoughts of his intended had something to do with it. Henry looked up at her.

"Yes, and I have a couple of patients to visit as well. Besides, your landlady was just popping out to the market when she let me in. If I'm still here when she gets back, she may start to suspect something."

"All right," Lydia sighed. "Show me what to do, then." She tapped at the typewriter keys.

"No, harder than that," Henry said. "It must make contact. Like this." He jabbed at the offending F, sending the little iron arm flying upwards. Obediently, Lydia hammered away at a few random keys.

She sucked her sore fingertip. "I'll have no hands to write with at this rate." Frowning, she looked at the blank sheet of paper. "So where's the words, then?"

"Ah." Reaching across, Henry lifted the bar that held the paper and wound the paper upwards. Sure enough, the line of gibberish she had typed was there, its imprint sharp and black on the virgin white sheet.

Lydia sniffed. "Understood."

"Oh, and I brought these, too." Henry set a small box on the bed beside her, and a potted plant in her lap. Baffled, she poked at one of the plant's shiny green leaves.

"What's that for?"

"It used to be in my workshop, didn't you notice it?"

"Can't say as I did."

"It's a bromeliad," Henry explained. "Most of them originated in the Americas, although this one's just a hybrid. They grow them in glasshouses in France nowadays, for people who want to keep them in their homes."

Lydia stuck her finger into the soil in the pot and stirred it around. The thought of paying a Frenchman to grow strange plants in pots perplexed her. "What am I s'posed to do with it?"

"It's just for decoration, to brighten the room up a bit. You'll have to remember to give it water, though."

She nodded, setting the plant down on the sill. "I see. Thanks."

She lifted the lid of the box, hoping it didn't contain one of Henry's specimen jars. A sheaf of thick paper printed with pictures lay inside, and Lydia flicked through them. Some pen and ink drawings, some smeary copies of paintings, even some taken with a camera like Henry's.

"Those are just some things I have left over. You can keep them if you like, or you can give them to John Fletcher when you next go that way. I'm sure he'll be able to sell them."

At the very back was one of his photographs of Lydia, stark naked, frozen like a sculpture.

"I thought you might like a picture of yourself, in case your readers start wondering who the mysterious 'Lancashire Rose' is." Henry winked.

"Very funny." Lydia tucked the portrait of herself

under her pillow and put the rest back into the box. "So you're really giving everything away, then?"

He sighed. "Everything except the camera, yes. My days as a pornographer are behind me, I'm afraid. It was cavalier—some might say foolish—of me to risk my reputation and my practice when I was a bachelor, but after tomorrow . . ." He held out his hands, staring blankly at his palms as if they held some secret.

"Oh aye, it's tomorrow, ain't it?"

"Yes. So you might as well have these. I have Pearl to think of, not to mention any . . ."

"Children."

"Yes. God, Lydia, I can't believe I'm doing this. I always believed that, by the time I came to wed, I would have some wisdom to pass on to my sons."

She nudged his hand with the backs of her fingers. "Well, you're doing what you can. You won't have your boxes of mucky pictures lying around for the little 'uns to find, so all you have to worry about now is explaining the jars of eyes and the boxes of human bones."

Henry shook his head, smiling. "You're a balm to ease all my worldly cares, my dear."

Henry soon hurried off to collect the new shirt and coat he'd ordered for his wedding. Reluctantly, Lydia pulled out the tatty scraps of paper on which she'd written her second edition of her gents' paper and set about thrashing out the new copy on the typewriter. By the time she'd finished, the sky had darkened with a murky blue dusk, and she ached from her fingers to her shoulders to her eyes. When Mrs. Bell called up the stairs, she jumped like a startled alley cat and bundled the pages away before the landlady could come up.

"Visitor for you, dear."

Henry again? As she hauled herself to her feet, though, she caught a strain of Mary's melodic, lilting Irish.

"You all right there?" Mrs. Bell called.

"This one?" came Mary's voice. "Yes, ta."

Lydia had reached her door before Mary had a chance to knock, and ushered her friend in, noticing with relief that she was wearing her light blue frock and no paint.

"Kathleen let you out, then?"

"I wanted to check you were managing. She wasn't too pleased about me going out, 'specially not to see you, but I talked her into it."

Lydia grimaced. "Here," she said, standing up and pulling her pink dress out of the wardrobe, "you'd best take this back with you."

"I'm not winding her up any more than I have to at the minute. You can take it back yourself—I've still got to live with her, remember."

"Aye," Lydia said guiltily, "I know, and I'm sorry.

You'd best not stay long. I'm surprised she don't think you're running away and all."

Mary looked down at her hands, folded in her lap. "Where would I go?" Tugging at Matty's cheap ring, she forced a smile. "Would you believe it, Kathleen was serious about Connie. Scrawny little cow's been set up in your old room."

"Never!"

"It's true, I swear. Herself told her not to eat too much; wants to keep her thin for them that likes a waif."

Finally, Lydia forced herself to ask the question she had been dreading.

"Have you heard from Matty, Mary?"

Tears glimmered in Mary's eyes, but she held her composure.

"I know they'll be putting him away when his trial comes," she whispered. "It's all I've thought about ever since he was arrested."

Lydia nodded helplessly, and Mary heaved a deep, shuddering sigh.

"And I know you said it'd cause me grief, but it weren't something I chose to do."

"I know. God's teeth, I'm not much better." Lydia waved her hand around at the little room, and Mary smiled comfortingly.

"Ah, you will cope, though. It's good what you've done: I'd like a place of my own as well some day." She took a deep breath. " 'Course, Matty's not likely to be there with me now—even if they let him out after a few years' hard labour. But I can make my plans for now. Save up a bit, like you did."

Lydia looked blankly at her friend. "Well, it sounds like you know what you're doing. You'll get there in the end, I reckon."

Mary nodded wearily. Out on the landing, Mrs. Bell's grandfather clock ticked away the minutes. The sound reminded Lydia of the clock outside her room at Kathleen's, and for a moment it was just as if she was back there, chatting in her room with Mary.

"And what about you, Lydia? Has Mr. Shadwell been round yet?"

"Aye."

Mary grinned. "You'll be a mistress yet."

"He's getting married tomorrow."

"It tends to be the married ones what have mistresses, don't it?"

Silence.

"Has Annie seen your new place?" Mary eventually asked. Lydia snorted.

"I saw her in the street but the little cow ran away 'cause I was talking to a man. Ashamed of her own sister, she is."

"Talking?" Mary smirked.

"Aye, talking, I swear. It was the bloke who prints up my papers. I've not seen her since."

Mary chuckled. "She don't change much, does she?"

"Life's a ladies' romance to her, I swear."

Mary nodded. "I remember once she asked me why I *liked* thrashing men, as if I woke up one morning and had a mind to do it."

Lydia chuckled. "Sod her. I've got more important things to worry about. Here, like my title?" She dropped to her knees and fished her copies of her paper out from under the bed.

"How should I know—what's it say?"

*"The White Flowers Reader."*

Mary paused, thinking, before laughing uproariously. Lydia smiled, relieved to hear Mary's merry cackle again.

"I wondered what you'd think of it. No one else seems to see the joke."

"I don't wonder. They'll either think that's the classiest thing they've ever heard or they'll know only a slut could've written it. I've got to hand it to you, Lydia, that's a good one. Oh God, I can't go giggling all the way back to Kathleen's or she really will think I'm up to something."

The next day Lydia found herself, almost against her will, standing outside St. John's. The wedding party had gone inside, leaving the carriage drivers outside to wait.

Lydia struggled to imagine Henry in there, standing side by side at the altar with his bride. That thought still needled Lydia, but she no longer felt the squeezing in her chest—as if her heart itself were being tightly laced—when she pictured Henry with the new Mrs. Shadwell: Pearl, like the earrings he had bought Lydia. The sense of freedom she felt was so new and strange that she couldn't help but revel in it, and she sighed as she leaned back against the wall around the front of the church. Despite the cold—and God knew how cruel this winter had been—she felt warm inside. Now the vicar's mumbling was giving way to a swell of organ music and a drone-like singing.

> *"Each little flower that opens,*
> *Each little bird that sings . . ."*

She knew this one. She'd sung it often enough back at the workhouse, usually before she'd been allowed to eat her breakfast. She thought she'd forgotten the words, but even those she couldn't hear from outside were coming back to her.

> *"The rich man in his castle,*
> *The poor man at his gate,*
> *He made them, high or lowly,*
> *And ordered their estate . . ."*

When she heard the rattle of the church door opening, she dragged herself away from the wall and stood further down the street, where she could easily slip into the crowd. There they were, in the shadow of the church porch: Henry, looking even more pressed and buttoned and groomed than usual; and a slender young woman with milky skin and brown hair a shade or so lighter than Lydia's. She was smiling shyly, but when Henry took her arm to lead her to the waiting carriage, she jumped at the unexpected touch, before correcting herself and nervously touching his fingertips with her own. Lydia chuckled. This looked as if it would be the honeymoon of most men's dreams (whether or not Henry was such a man was another matter, Lydia thought). The driver had climbed down and was holding the door open for Pearl. Lydia stretched up on the tips of her toes and raised her head, allowing Henry to catch sight of her, before strolling smoothly towards the wedding party as if she'd never seen either the bride or groom in her life. She suppressed a smirk as Henry winked at her before hopping into the carriage after his wife.

She turned back and headed for home after that, stopping to buy three cakes from a baker's lad with a tray. Her leg ached in the cold, but it was no less intoxicating to be out in town, free to do as she pleased without the knowledge that she would have to return to Kathleen's. Having bought three hair-ribbons from the market, she strolled back in the direction of the station and Mrs. Bell's.

She noticed a crowd gathering just ahead. Something had clearly stirred them, and Lydia idly wondered if someone had been caught thieving. The last time she'd seen this kind of commotion was when a lad had been found with a pocket-watch he'd stolen. She elbowed her way through the rabble, stopping in her tracks when she saw that the crowd was staring as one at something high above.

Annabel was perched on a ledge under the rooftop of the Baptist church. She stood clasping the chiselled stone, resisting the pulling of the winter winds. The hem of her dress looked ragged, perhaps torn during the climb. In the street below, the crowd watched open-mouthed, some of the better-dressed women stealing one-eyed glimpses as they buried their faces in their husbands' shoulders.

All that Lydia could muster was a wordless bellow that strained the back of her throat. She stared mutely at Annie, whose pink face trembled in fear as she shifted her stockinged feet on the narrow stone ledge; she must have taken her boots off before she began the climb. She almost lost her footing, and Lydia could just about hear her shriek as it was blown away by the wind. Forcing her way between the strangers in the crowd, Lydia pushed her way to the front, where Annie would be able to see her. The wind blew hard.

"Annie!" she yelled. Annabel didn't even flinch.

"Annabel!" No sooner was the name out of her mouth than it happened. Annabel let go of the stonework and allowed herself to fall forward, her arms outstretched, her eyes facing straight ahead as she sailed downwards.

It felt as though she'd knelt beside Annie's dumb, gaping form for days when the law arrived. It couldn't have been all that long, really—they were only a pair of coppers strolling up Fishergate, and they looked as surprised at the sight of the prim, well-groomed young suicide as anyone else, but they soon took charge of the situation, one ordering the crowd back, while the other tried to draw Lydia away. For a while she didn't even acknowledge him, but the pain when he made to haul her to her feet forced her to wrestle her arm out of his grasp and turn on him.

"She's my bloody sister!"

Aside from the horrible mess of her face, Annie looked almost grotesquely proper, save for the tears in her skirts and a couple of buttons at the neck of her dress that had come loose, leaving exposed a flash of white throat that was prim by Lydia's standards, but which Annabel would never have been seen showing when she was alive. Then Lydia saw it—a sharp, bright white corner poking out from the front of Annie's dress: a slip of paper tucked down into her underthings.

"Come now, Miss." A peeler pulled her to her feet. In a heartbeat, she reached out and snatched the paper from Annie's dress and shoved it into her own pocket.

# 19

Lydia,

*This letter was meant for you, even if you never receive it. If you have been told that I took my own life, then it is not a scandal. I am sorry, sister, but it is true. I thought here to explain my reasons, but I fear it would all be for nought, for how do we ever understand a person's reasons for doing what I will have done by the time this letter reaches you? Particularly when one considers the differences in character between us— indeed, it is these differences that have brought my time here on Earth to this most unhappy end.*

*Lydia, I cannot face another day. I do so admire your ability to endure, for as the Lord (may He show me mercy) is my witness, I know that I would have no need to compose this letter if endurance were a gift I shared with you. I wish that I could have been more like you.*

*I have contracted an unspeakable illness, Lydia. I put such effort into my studies at school, and I have tried so very hard in my position as Governess to Lavinia and Lilia, but still I have been dishonoured and diseased, just as I would have been had I stayed at Kathleen's . . .*

*Henry, where are you?*

Lydia knew the answer, of course—he'd have set off on his honeymoon. She wasn't going to find him at his workshop, or in one of the local pubs.

Arriving at the boarding-house, she had walked straight up to her room as if in an opium daze. She couldn't remember the walk back from town, or even unlocking the front door of the house. Her hands and feet hadn't felt like her own, and she had fumbled with her bedroom doorkey, unable to keep a proper grasp. Then she had fallen to her knees, barely managing to pull the pot out from under her bed before regurgitating the half-digested cream cake, followed by a stream of bile that burned her throat, sending her whole body into convulsions as she huddled over the pot.

Even when she had locked the door, she had felt vulnerable and exposed. Only when she had shoved the heavy typewriter in front of the door had she pulled Annie's letter from her pocket and huddled into a ball on the bed. Her fingers trembled as she turned the envelope over.

Annie's neat script may have been very different to Lydia's own sharp Ls, and her Ys with the flouncy, curly tails, but even as she'd written her final letter her hand had been fastidiously clear and precise. She had addressed the envelope to Lydia at her new accommodation at Mrs. Bell's: Annie had clearly read Lydia's final letter to her, even if she had not replied.

Lydia read on.

> *The fault is my employer's—Mr. Hollingworth— and thus I fear that this letter may be destroyed before you have an opportunity to read it. At first I told myself that I was imagining his advances, that watching the men who visited you and the other girls at Kathleen's had made me falsely fear lechery from all the male sex. Yet he became bolder, and by the time I had accepted that I should indeed be fearful, it was too late—I had been violated. It has continued for at least a month now.*
>
> *I cannot continue. I cannot endure one more time: ignoring the pain and wishing it away; the shame of my body being given over to that man;*

*the always-dashed hope that it will not happen again, or that I am merely dreaming and will soon awaken to a better day. I have considered coming to you for help—I have even set out to visit you and explain my troubles—but what, after all, would you be able to do? How might you be able to rescue another from a life you yourself live?*

*Oh, listen to me—I cannot stop myself from talking even now. I always did talk a great deal, didn't I? There is something comforting in words, and I think you may understand, even though you are not a scholar, for I do remember how well you took to reading and writing. So many things seem much smaller when one describes them in words, but not this. My favoured defence against pain has failed me at the last, for how can words save me from a life I can no longer live?*

*I know that it is not customary for you to do so, but please pray for me, Lydia. After God's mercy, it is my only hope.*

*Your sister,*
*Annabel*

Lydia's jaw tightened, and the page of Annabel's careful script shook in her hand. She read over the neat lines of handwriting again and again: *I have been dishonoured and diseased, just as I would have been had I stayed at Kathleen's.* Rage and sorrow and pity welled up in her throat. Sitting up and crumpling the letter into a tight ball in her fist, she hurled it at the window, a guttural cry of fury escaping her when it bounced smoothly off the glass and pattered to the floor, as if shattering glass would have comforted her somehow.

Giving in to the suffocating feeling that burned the backs of her eyes and pressed down on her huddled form, Lydia sobbed until her throat was so swollen and hoarse that she could only lie mute on the bed, staring levelly at the ball of paper on the floor, as cool and impassive as death itself, while hot tears ran down her face, dropping off her cheeks and dampening her mattress. *If I had gone to find her before now, even just this morning ...* It was all useless. She *hadn't* gone to find Annie and she *hadn't* offered her a home in her new lodgings; and now she never could.

Lydia closed her eyes in desperation, trying to halt the strange whirling sensation inside her head. Even lying down, she felt dizzy. A memory flickered in her mind: the day after Jimmy had eaten the poison bait, all those years ago in the workhouse. Lydia had gone outside as usual after prayers and breakfast to collect more chips of stone in her basket, and as she made her way around the workyard, she had caught sight of the corner where Jimmy had found the tainted bacon. She had stared blankly at the ground, wondering why he had not known—as Nell had claimed everyone did—about the poisoned scraps being left out for the rats. That evening, over supper, she had asked her mother, but Nell had shrugged Lydia's queries off.

Bile rose in Lydia's throat. She should have found someone; told them that the poisoned bacon was there and that someone might eat it. If she had, Jimmy might have lived to see another year; or even to see manhood, just as Lydia had grown into a woman. But she had believed her mother and held her tongue, and Jimmy had died for it. And now Annie, too. All Lydia's daydreams of storming into the Hollingworth house and dragging her sister away were useless now. It was too late. She would never argue with Annabel again, and she'd never know whether she could have saved her. Her face felt stiff, and her eyes stung from weeping.

She sat bolt upright. Poison. She remembered what Nell had told them all those years ago: a few flypapers were enough, if you knew what you were doing. Life was fragile: far more so than folk realized, but Lydia knew it well enough now.

Before she could look again at the crumpled-up letter, before she could sink again under a torrent of despair, she stood up and headed for the door. If she allowed herself to pause now, she would never act.

# 20

The flypapers were easy to find. King's ironmongers had boxes full of them. She took three, neatly rolled into little tubes and wrapped in butcher paper, then paused before grabbing a handful more. Three might kill a rat, but she couldn't assume they would suit her purpose. She paid for them at the till, and Miss King hadn't batted an eyelid. Back in her room, Lydia watched the little strips of paper bobbing on the surface of the pitcher of water she'd taken from Mrs. Bell's kitchen while the old woman dozed into her chest in the parlour. The water was slowly turning milky, white particles swirling and eddying like tealeaves. She watched the brewing poison with care, not allowing herself to think beyond the next minute. Gradually, she ceased to hear the noise of the street below and the ticking of Mrs. Bell's grandfather clock. Then a sound shattered the silence, and her heart lurched. There was someone thumping at her door.

With a start, Lydia scraped her hair away from her face. Had she imagined it? No. There it was again. In a panic, she fished the sodden strips of paper from the jug and scrunched them into a ball, before wiping her hands on her skirt.

"Lydia!" It was Mary.

"Miss Ketch? You've got a visitor, poppet, open up now." Mrs. Bell. *Poppet?* Mary must have heard about Annie and told Mrs. Bell.

"Lydia, I know you're in there," Mary was saying.

After another glance at the jug of water, she finally pushed the typewriter and the bundle of wet flypapers under the bed and fumbled with the lock.

"Ah, there you are, dear." Mrs. Bell hoisted Jonah under one arm. "Your friend's here. How's about I bring the two of you a nice cup of tea?"

Before Lydia could answer, Mary squeezed past Mrs. Bell into Lydia's room.

"That'd be lovely, Mrs. Bell. Thank you."

The landlady turned and headed back down the stairs.

"Mother, I thought she'd never leave," Mary muttered, shutting the door. She stopped, looking at Lydia perched on the bed. It occurred to Lydia that she probably looked half-mad or on the verge of leaping off a building herself.

"Lydia . . ." Mary's cornflower eyes were huge and pleading, silently begging Lydia to help her find some words that would help. Lydia looked back at her silently. She could hear Mrs. Bell's grandfather clock again.

"How'd you find out?" she sighed.

"Connie, the little gobshite. She was shopping in town and apparently it's all anyone's talking about. She told me and Kathleen as soon as she got back." She paused, scrutinizing Lydia. "She said that a governess had thrown herself from the church: someone who worked for a quality family on the square. I knew before she said it that the family would be the Hollingworths."

Hearing the man's name sent a wave of nausea over Lydia, and the first time she tried to speak about Annie's note, she had to stop for dry retching. She gulped hard, fighting down her need to spit.

"It were his fault," she whispered through cracked lips. "She left this. I had to steal the fucking thing from inside her dress; I've no idea who she thought would've found it if I hadn't been there. The law would've opened it if I hadn't seen it first, and I don't imagine they'd have bothered to send it on to me when they were done." She pushed Annie's screwed-up note across the bed, and Mary picked it up even though Lydia knew she couldn't read. Mary smoothed the paper out on her lap, pressing it flat with her hands.

"What's it say?" One hand was palm-down on the lines of writing.

"She . . ." Lydia faltered. "He forced himself on her."

"Aye." There was no surprise in Mary's voice.

"I should have seen it coming . . . She wanted quality living to be different. She thought men with money were different."

Mary shook her head.

"She was only at Kathleen's a year." Lydia flopped back onto the bed. Her clothes felt sour, as if she'd been wearing them for a week, and she folded her arms across her aching eyes. "I would've thought she'd have learned in that time, though. But she was just a kid; I shouldn't have let her leave, Mary. She needed me."

"How would you have stopped her? She was determined. You could hardly have gone with her." Mary pulled one of Lydia's arms away from her face, and Lydia yanked it back. She needed the darkness and the closeness, and the feel of her sleeves, smooth against her damp skin.

"It's my fault," she said. "It never felt right when she left, even though part of me was happy to see the back of her. I knew she'd come a cropper, I knew she'd no more make a quality servant than I would. I even wanted her to run into a bit of trouble, to tell the truth. That it'd stop her looking at me the way she did."

She drew a shuddering breath.

"Not like this, though. I never wanted this. I should've done something or said something. It were all spite: I didn't protect her like I should have out of spite for Ma and all her grand ideas about how Annie was the one with the makings of someone special." Lydia balled her fists, digging her long fingernails into her palms. "But Ma's dead, ain't she?" Lydia looked pleadingly at Mary. "Has been for nearly two years now, and now Annie's dead too, 'cause all I could think of was Ma being wrong. I've won, I was right. And my sister died to prove me right."

Mary looked blankly around the room. Then she pursed her lips.

"What's this, Lydia?" She was looking at the pitcher of cloudy water beside the bed.

Lydia felt light-headed. "It's arsenic," she said, before cringing and lowering her voice. "They used to use it in the workhouse on the rats and that." Her voice sounded strange, as if she were reading her own words from a book.

"You were never going to do yourself in?"

Lydia choked a little. "No, you silly cow. I . . ."

Mary's lips parted ever so slightly. "You mean it's for Hollingworth? Christ, Lydia, I never thought you'd be so stupid."

"He killed my fucking sister, or as good as!" Lydia hissed.

"If you want to die, Lydia, why not just do it now?"

"I don't want to die!"

"Then why are you setting yourself up for the rope? How are you going to do it without anyone seeing you?

Without anyone suspecting? Without the law finding you out?"

"I don't know."

"It don't matter that he deserves to die for what he done; he won't, or if he does, you will too. D'you think they'll care why you did it? The likes of us can't afford justice."

Standing up and pacing the room, Lydia fought to keep her voice down. "Annie was different, Mary. She weren't one of us. I told you, she wanted life to be a storybook."

"It runs in the family."

Lydia started to protest, but Mary shook her head.

"You're playing the little romantic heroine now, ain't you?"

All the strength went from Lydia's body, and she let herself sag and drop back down onto the bed. Mary ran her fingers through her tangled hair.

"You're right, true enough. But you know what it's like—look at you and Matty! Where was all this sensible talk then?"

"Coming from you, as I recall." A single tear fell down Mary's cheek, and she swept it away with the back of her hand. "And Matty got cocky and now he's in prison, and I've no idea what I'll do with myself, but at least I shan't be dying in the hangman's noose. You've got the new home and the new life you wanted. Don't throw it away now; it won't make a scrap of difference to Annie. We'll go down the church if you like and say some prayers for her soul, but don't you go dying and all. I need you, too, Lydia."

Something in her friend's voice touched a nerve deep inside Lydia; one she doubted that all Henry's books and anatomical diagrams could have named. She sighed heavily, and her ribs ached as if they had been kicked. Mary stood up and shoved the pitcher of arsenic-laced water into her hand. "Give it the plant."

Lydia snatched the jug, and the whitish water drenched the soil in the plant pot.

## 21

The headstone over Annabel's grave bore only her name.
The soil was still soft and freshly turned as Lydia knelt by
the graveside and laid a single white lily on the earth.

"They were never going to give you a Christian burial,
were they?" she said quietly. "But it's not a bad spot.
Peaceful." She looked across the graveyard, towards the
busy rows of stones marking graves on the sanctified
area. From Annabel's graveside, over at the edge of the
cemetery with the unbaptized babies and the dissenters
and the other suicides, she could barely see the grave
where Daisy now rested. She stared at her knees pressing
into the wet grass and thought of the layers of earth below, and of the cheap, flimsy coffin the undertaker had

recommended. Annie's shattered body was barely a few feet beneath her.

"You never did understand that I didn't do it for the good of me health, did you?" she whispered, twining a hank of her hair around her fingers again and again. "I could've done better by you, Annie, and I'm sorry I didn't." Tears sprang to her eyes, and she swept her fingers along her lashes, trying to stop her paint from running. "God, you silly little bitch—why didn't you just come to me?"

She fell silent, composing herself. Above, the lonesome cawing of the crows in the trees continued implacably. When Lydia spoke again, her voice was little more than a thread.

"I thought about fixing him. It seemed like the right thing to do; it's what they always do in stories, ain't it? Someone gets killed, someone they know has to take revenge; always works that way." Lydia reached out and caressed the lily lying on the grave. She was loath to leave it there; to abandon it at the cemetery along with the remains of her sister. She had clung to Annie's letter, too: sleeping with it under her pillow until she had made up her mind. Then she had dropped it through the letterbox at the police station before making her way to visit her sister; the worn and tearstained letter slipping from her fingers and into an uncertain fate.

"But where does it get people like us, acting like we fell out of a storybook? Mary had it right—kicking about on the end of a rope is where it'd get me."

Lydia looked one more time at the headstone. "I'm sorry, Annie. Best go now. Love you."


A week later, with the second edition of *The White Flowers Reader* delivered safely to Stan, Lydia hurried back to Mrs. Bell's, an ink-blue shawl huddled around her shoulders to keep out the cold of the lingering winter. It was the darkest garment she owned, and she'd promised herself she'd wear it in honour of Annie.

"Lydia!" The familiar voice made her jump. Securing her shopping basket on her arm, she turned to face the voice.

"Kathleen." A train pulled out from the station below, and Kathleen wafted away the cloud of smoke.

"Connie told us about Annie."

"Aye." Lydia gritted her teeth. "I ain't freezing my arse out here, so you'll have to walk with us if you want to keep talking." Tucking her hands back under her shawl, she continued on her way. Behind her, she heard Kathleen grumble, but the abbess followed her and caught up.

"Lyd—" Kathleen's voice started off harsh, but for the first time since she'd known her, Lydia heard her stop and moderate her tone. "*Lydia*, I'm sorry it happened. I understand what you've been thinking. I had a few thoughts like that myself."

Lydia stopped still, her eyes wide. "What d'you mean?"

"Mary told us you blamed yourself for what your sister done, that you thought you could've stopped her."

Putting her head down, Lydia closed her eyes and let Kathleen's words wash over her.

"She'd never have stayed on as a maid at my place . . ."

"Aye, I know. She just had a mind to do what she wanted to do and that was that." She stopped outside Mrs. Bell's front door, and dug around in her pocket for the key.

"You'd best not come in. I don't think the landlady'd approve."

Kathleen grinned. "More fool her."

"But wait here: I've got that dress you gave me. I don't want to be in debt to you or anyone else."

"It's only one frock," Kathleen said dismissively. "Keep it."

"It was the only one you ever bought for me. The other abbesses buy all their girls' clothes."

The older woman was quiet for some time, but eventually she spoke.

"I had to run away from my old house in a dress my abbess bought me. I could cope with her anger and the threat of a beating; I could cope with finding my way to a new town; but I kept meself awake at night thinking about what might happen if she got the law on me for thieving a poxy dress. I parcelled it up and sent it back to her once I got settled in Preston, would you believe it?" Kathleen hesitated. She looked embarrassed now by her confession. "All that fuss," she said, shaking her head, "all that fuss just to say I had a house of my own. But I'll tell you this, there's nowhere on God's earth that don't have a use for an introduction house."

Lydia smiled. "You know, that's what I got from you, Kathleen: it's best to make your money from something that'll always be with us."

"Like your gents' papers, I s'pose?" Kathleen said wryly.

"Exactly." Lydia grinned impishly as another thought occurred to her. "Tell you what, how's about we stay in business together? D'you fancy selling some copies of *The White Flowers Reader*?"

Kathleen raised an eyebrow. "That depends. Do I get any for meself?"

Lydia suppressed a smile. "I'll give you a couple for the parlour."

Kathleen spat into her palm and held out her hand for Lydia to shake.

"Then it's settled."


That evening, Lydia sat cross-legged on her narrow bed, drafting a story in pen and ink. Her fingers were streaked with ink.

"Lydia! Your surgeon to see you!"

She was still wondering when Mrs. Bell would become suspicious about the number of visitors she had been receiving, but the landlady seemed to think this was normal, for "a young lady today," as she put it.

"S'open!" she called out as Henry tapped at the door.

"Still no chairs," she said, gesturing for him to sit down on the bed. Her gaze drifted intuitively towards his left hand, and Lydia noticed that he had chosen not to wear a wedding ring. Still, rings were probably impractical for a man in Henry's line of work.

"I'll manage. Gracious, what on earth happened to my bromeliad?" He pointed at the limp, shrivelled stem poking out of the pot of soil, and Lydia caught her breath.

"I've never been any good at looking after things. I keep meaning to chuck it out."

Henry's smile faltered, and he looked hesitantly at Lydia. "I called in on some of my patients yesterday. Including the Hollingworth child."

Lydia fell silent.

"I was told about your sister. I'm truly sorry. Perhaps if I had spoken to her on one of my visits . . ."

Lydia shook her head. "I've been through all that myself. She's . . ." Her voice wavered, but she licked her lips and forced herself to say it. "She's dead, and there's no changing it."

Henry hooked his smallest finger around Lydia's, and she was grateful that he'd not taken her in his arms. She doubted she could have held her composure.

"Say no more."

"Well, I'm not sitting here in silence!"

"I must confess silence would be quite welcome. Pearl appears to have found her voice. I've heard about nothing but end tables and silverware."

Lydia chuckled. "Still," she said, "your virgin bride must have her compensations."

"Oh yes. I shouldn't disparage her—she's a personable enough girl. But I have started to miss the company of someone who is a little more . . . worldly."

"Is that a fancy word for a slag?"

Henry smiled his infectious smile.

"You knew I wasn't marrying Pearl because she was my ideal companion."

Lydia nodded. "Aye, I know. Who you marry ain't my business, and I've got my own life to live. I mean, this place might not be much"—she gestured at the room around them—"but it's mine, or as close to mine as I can get."

"Yes. I have to say I've never known another woman quite like you, Lydia. When we first met, I used to wonder if you'd have been happier had you been born a man, but now I see you've done pretty well as you are." He paused, reaching into his pocket and retrieving a folded paper. As he flattened it out across his knee, Lydia caught her breath: it was the first edition of *The White Flowers Reader*. Henry smiled.

"Do you remember when we first met, and I told your abbess about an acquaintance of mine? The old school friend?"

Lydia screwed up her face momentarily as she thought back. "Aye—the collector, wasn't he?"

"That's the one. Well, I sent him a copy of your paper, and he was intrigued. At his request, I obtained a few more for him, and he believes that he would be able to distribute your paper to some of the booksellers he knows in Manchester and Wigan. In time, perhaps further afield as well."

Lydia's eyes were wide. "He's going to help me sell my paper?" Her voice trembled, and her throat tightened. She had never wept with happiness in her life, but now she wondered if this was what it might feel like when you came close.

"Yes, and you couldn't ask for a better man to help. He knows the trade inside and out, and he certainly helped me to sell more of my photographs than I imagine I would have otherwise. Oh, I forgot—I brought you these." He laid a soft parcel in Lydia's lap, and she tore the paper off. Inside was a set of neatly folded white linen bedding: the lace-trimmed sheets that had adorned the bed back at Henry's workshop. She smiled and thanked him as she shook them out, draping them over the pile of old clothes covering her mattress.

Henry caught her around the waist as she fussed with her new bedcovers. "Am I permitted to continue visiting?"

Lydia chewed her lip. She was silent for a moment, and when she spoke again, her voice was thin and child-like.

"I s'pose so, but there's to be no more talk of corpses, Henry. Please." She had made her lip bleed now, and she rubbed the back of her hand against her mouth. "I've had a bellyful of death."

Henry nodded as his arms wrapped around her.